Prairie Ghosts

WHITE RAVEN SERIES BOOK I

AnneMarie Dapp

D1546448

PRAIRIE GHOSTS
Copyright © 2020 by AnneMarie Dapp

ISBN: 978-1-68046-872-4

Published by Satin Romance
An Imprint of Melange Books, LLC
White Bear Lake, MN 55110
www.satinromance.com

Published in the United States of America.

Cover Design by Ashley Redbird Designs

For Dale

Humankind has not woven the web of life. We are but one thread within it. Whatever we do to the web, we do to ourselves. All things are bound together. All things connect.

— *CHIEF SEATTLE, DUWAMISH (1780–1866)*

Chapter One

CATHY WHISPERED A PRAYER FOR HER MOTHER.
Amber light washed over the grave as a trail of fire ants inched along the curve of the mound. Raindrops darkened the dusty earth. Bare feet followed a worn path leading toward the main road. The cedar chest was found where she'd left it, covered in a blanket of dew. Hastily, she clicked open the lock, searching frantically for her boots. Sighing in relief, she discovered them buried underneath an old shift. The remaining possessions were sorted and stacked inside the wooden container. She counted: three homespun dresses, her diary, the family Bible, needles and thread, scissors, undergarments, linen, a Sunday bonnet, and several glass jars filled with dried herbs. Her fingers grazed over the collection of medicinal plants. *I'll need to collect more on the road.*

The pounding of hoofbeats woke her from her musings. Her neighbor maneuvered the team along the path, the morning sun highlighting his blond waves, a carefree grin moving over his face. He pulled up alongside the supplies and climbed down. His manner was casual, but his eyes couldn't quite hide his concern.

"Sorry to be running late. You're going to get drenched in this weather. That's no way to start a journey."

He offered his arm, guiding her to the front rig under the protection of a covered awning. The team blew tendrils of steam into the misty air. The molly whinnied, while her partner nipped playfully at her shoulder. Stocky mules struck the ground, anxious to be on their way. Tethered alongside the frisky pair was an appaloosa gelding. The young man gave the horse a gentle pat before lifting the hope chest underneath the covered wagon. Barrels of dried beans, lentils, barley, fruits, vegetables, and barrels of rainwater were stacked together. Tin mugs, bowls, and cooking utensils filled an ancient-looking cauldron. In the opposite corner sat a Cherrywood vanity—a beloved heirloom passed down from her great-grandmother. A hay-filled mattress took up the remaining space. Handmade quilts covered the modest bed.

"Took me a little longer than I expected, my dear. I replaced the back left wheel and axle, along with the front board. So, I went ahead and fixed them both. Should hold well now."

"You're always so thoughtful. Mighty obliged, Shane."

He looked at her carefully; the soft morning light mirrored in his steel-gray eyes.

"Are you sure this is what you want to do, Cat? An unescorted woman on the trail might be inviting trouble. I'll be tied up working the cattle drive most days. I won't always be close. Oh, and I almost forgot, the sheriff assigned me guard duty starting tonight." He trailed off, realizing her mind was elsewhere.

She gazed out at the prairie; her jaw set firmly. "Appreciate it, but I'll manage. Some of our neighbors will be traveling the same route. They can help me, I imagine."

"You've always been a stubborn one." His smile brought out his dimples, but his face grew serious as he looked back at the wagon. "I spoke to the MacGregors yesterday. They've invited you to travel with um' and set up camp. Both are elderly, but Mr. MacGregor has his guns, and his eyes are still sharp." He hesitated before saying, "I'd feel better if you'd take them up on their offer."

She nodded absently, looking toward the mountains. He wondered if she was even listening.

"I'll try to check up on you when I can."

Climbing back into the rig, he took the reins; a light flick and they were on their way. They rode in silence, each trying to work out their uncertain futures in their minds. When they arrived at the Platte River, they noticed countless numbers of travelers preparing for the journey. A quick-moving current flowed over the winding curves of the valley. The darkening sky made the river appear eerily dense.

A long line of wagons already arrived. Several children played by the water searching for frogs and lizards by the murky bank. Their playful laughter seemed out of place somehow. A young mother called out to her brood. They either didn't hear or chose to ignore her. She tottered down the hill, hand clutching her swollen belly. Cathy wondered how traveling might be for a pregnant woman.

Scattered across the prairie were several thousand long-steer cattle. The herd would follow the wagon train to Monterey. Most were rust-colored with patches of white. A few Angus bulls stood in contrast, their coal-black hides appearing like sinister shadows.

A group of young men oversaw scouting missions, which consisted in searching for suitable camping sites, water sources, and trading posts. Some took on the added duty of security, being first responders to call attention to any dangerous or suspicious activities along the way. Shane volunteered to work the cattle drive and help with scouting duty. The pay was modest, but the extra money would help him get down to the California territory where he could start his life anew.

The wranglers would have their hands busy keeping the herd together. Bandits and thieves would not be tolerated. Cathy studied the cattle stretched across the vast prairie, wandering the hillside. Men rode along the plains on horseback, shouting commands, guiding the animals behind the caravan. Departure time was close.

Shane climbed out of the wagon and offered his hand. He concentrated on her features, trying to memorize every detail. Dark curls floated past her shoulders, pooling around a heart-shaped face. Emerald eyes framed by ebony lashes, pupils dilating under the rising sun—a startling combination of innocence and pain. A hesitant smile flickered. She blushed, looking down at her worn boots, delicate hands fidgeting with the edges of her sunbonnet. Although small and calloused, her fingers were nimble with a needle and able to wield the plow when needed. A scattering of freckles across her golden skin attested to the long hours spent outside tilling the soil, easing its rich bounty from the red earth. She would miss the land, but it held too much sorrow, too many memories…and ghosts.

She gazed upwards.

"Thank you for everything. I wish you luck and safety on your travels."

His face grew serious as he untethered his pony. With a tilt of his hat, horse and rider disappeared into the heavy mist. After he was gone, Cathy sat back in the wagon seat and closed her eyes. Time drifted. A warm breeze caressed her face as the rain tapered to a drizzle. A congress of ravens descended from the hazy sky landing on the trees along the bank—their shiny wings glistening in the morning dew.

The landscape appeared dotted by thousands of dark spirits. Multitudes of birds perched in the willow trees, their inky eyes seeming to follow her every move. Mules were anxious, striking the ground, muscles twitching, and in an instant, the ravens took flight, their bodies coming together like an ominous shadow disappearing into the heavens.

One juvenile bird remained. It thrashed the ground trying in vain to fly; the right wing bent at a startling angle. Agitated by the bird's plight, the team hawed and stamped. Leaving the rig, Cathy climbed down to get a closer look. She patted the john mule's flank, and he ceased fidgeting. She tentatively reached her hand toward the frightened creature. His shiny eyes caught her gaze, and she knew in an instant what she must do.

Cradling him close, they headed back to her wagon where she rummaged through her hope chest in search of fabric. She used a small piece of cotton linen to wrap his wing in place. Surprisingly, the bird remained still, his eyes searching her face inquisitively. She placed the remaining cloth inside a wooden bowl as a makeshift nest. Once settled, he nibbled the soft material, fluffed his feathers, and began to preen.

Satisfied, she examined her collection of dried herbs. She chose a combination of wheat grain, barley, parsley, and thyme grinding them firmly into her pestle. A drizzle of honey was mixed in, forming a rich paste. She offered the raven a few drops of water and feed, which he devoured. The creature's eyes closed, his ebony beak resting against his chest. When he was asleep, she placed the bird and nest on top of the straw mattress.

Outside, the winds were strengthening—flashes of lightning streaking across the amber sky. Horses reared and stomped as thunder rolled off in the distance. From the seemingly endless throng of travelers appeared a tall gentleman on horseback. Flecks of gray peppered his jet-black hair; his face tan and weathered, worry lines etched deep around his eyes and mouth. He rode a palomino gelding, guiding him to the top of the ravine, stopping to survey the prairie schooners.

"Good morning, travelers!"

His voice was commanding, the sound echoing down the valley and river. A few men called back, answering him by name.

"Many of you know me. We've been neighbors and friends for many years. For those who don't, my name's David Carpenter. I'm the sheriff of these parts. I've been asked to lead this wagon train, and I've accepted the job and will do my best to serve our community. A group of us will be surveying the land, scouting for water sources, looking out for cattle thieves, and the like."

A murmur went through the crowd as he spoke. He let it die down before he continued.

"I'd like to explain a few things about our journey. We'll be traveling northwestward, our final destinations being Oregon, San Francisco, and Monterey. Some of you may not make it all the way for this will not be an easy trip. We'll be dealing with the unknown—the elements often unpredictable, food and water sometimes scarce. Scouts will ride on ahead, searching for the best rest stops, looking out for possible bandits."

A nervous chatter ran through the crowd.

"Our caravan will stop twice a day—once for lunch and a second time for supper and camp. I suggest preparing simple meals for breakfast since we will be leaving at dawn's first light. A horn will be sounded at noon and again at suppertime. Bullwhackers will help chain the wagons together at sunset each evening. Stray cattle will be corralled inside these barriers, keeping them safe from predators and thieves. Once the wagons are tied, it will be important to stay inside the safety of the corral. Guards will be posted at outposts every evening around the wagon train. They'll keep an eye out for any dangers in the night. These duties will be switched out on the third week of each month, so men, make sure to check-in for your assigned schedule.

"We will be facing many obstacles, but it's important to remember the people of Nebraska are tough. We've been through good times and bad crop failures, illness, and natural disasters. We'll face these new challenges together as we've done in the past. Now, I'd like to invite Father Sebastian to come up and say a few words."

An elderly priest walked toward the crowd, his baby blue eyes sparkling in the morning sun. The crowd greeted him warmly, many calling him "Father."

"Good morning, friends!" His manner was calm, his voice kind and inviting. With a thick Irish brogue, he addressed the travelers.

"I've known many of you since you were wee babes." Several travelers waved and signaled from the crowd.

"I want to tell you the Lord will be with us along this great journey. Take peace in knowing God's eyes are watching us even now. I'll be leading Sunday Mass each week and will be available for confessions and Bible study for those interested.

"Some of you may not be Catholic, and it's all right. Everyone is invited. No one will be turned away, as we're all God's children. For the people traveling to Monterey, I'll be helping to set up a new Mission there. It's my hope and prayer to bring the word of Jesus Christ to those new to our faith. Blessed be the souls yet to hear his beautiful voice and speak his glorious name. Good news is coming. Hallelujah!"

An excited murmur ran through the crowd. Fathers held their children high on their shoulders to get a better view of their beloved priest.

"Well now, I'd like you all to hold hands as we recite the Lord's Prayer."

Husbands and wives, brothers and sisters joined hands with one another. He made the sign of the cross, "In the name of the Father, the Son, and the Holy Spirit,

Our Father,
Who art in heaven,
hallowed be Thy name;
Thy kingdom come;
Thy will be done on earth as it is in heaven.
Give us this day our daily bread;
and forgive us our trespasses
as we forgive those who trespass against us;
and lead us not into temptation,
but deliver us from evil. Amen."

Afterward, the crowd greeted him with kind words. He headed into the throng of travelers, shaking hands and offering blessings.

Sheriff Carpenter moved toward the platform to address the people once more.

"Let's begin our journey, friends."

He held a large bull horn to the sky and blew deeply. The repercussion echoed across the valley. Men called out to the line of wagons signaling their departure. Cowboys whooped and hollered guiding their cattle westward.

Chapter Two

DUST SWIRLED IN TRANSIENT CLOUDS POWDERING THE WAGONS, THE travelers, their clothes, and bedding. The powder was everywhere and in everything. A gritty taste clung to Cathy's tongue as sweat trickled down the small of her back. The warm breeze blew her hair into her eyes, so she fastened her long curls into a ponytail. She reached for her canteen, pulling the cork out with her back teeth, rinsed the sand out of her mouth. The wagon bumped and swayed over the rolling prairie, luring her into a meditative state. There were seemingly endless miles to travel before the bull horn sounded for their last stop of the day. As they drew close to the silty waters of the Platte River, Cathy maneuvered her wagon alongside the MacGregor's and waited for further instructions.

Wranglers made their way around camp on horseback explaining to the pioneers how to hitch their wagons together in a large oval loop. Afterward, the men went about tying the prairie schooners together with chains, sometimes metal rods. This would serve as a kind of makeshift corral which would contain some of the unrulier cattle in at night. The barrier also allowed extra protection from possible outside dangers.

As the cowboys assisted the travelers in setting up camp, Cathy freed her mules from their tethers, and then led them toward the riverbank to graze. They dropped their heads and immediately started nibbling at the sweet sage grass. Once they were settled, she wandered over toward a cluster of birch trees. Colorful wildflowers covered the ground along with many native plants rich in color and variety. With an expert eye, she searched for stinging nettles. Cotton gloves protected her skin from the harsh oils as she placed the leaves into her basket and headed toward camp. Mr. MacGregor was helping his wife down from the wagon. Her face appeared quite pale; gray hair pulled back in a large bun. A flowered shift fluttered loosely around her plump frame. She moved slowly, but with a quiet determination, a light film of sweat on her brow and a soft smile on her face.

"Ah, Cathy, so nice to see you again. Been awhile. Guess the last time was at your ma's funeral…"

The elderly woman changed the subject. "Mr. MacGregor will be fetching some firewood if you'd care to make camp with us, dear."

Cathy glanced over at her gnarled hands, noticing the slight tremor and swollen knuckles.

"I'd love to."

"Why don't you come on over and we can make a nice tea together."

"You read my mind. I just finished collecting some fresh nettles. Figured it might help with our aches and pains from traveling."

Mrs. MacGregor smiled, realizing the nettles were for her benefit.

"Sounds mighty smart."

Mr. MacGregor collected branches by a grove of spindly trees near the south bank of the river. He busied himself preparing the cooking fire, while the women planned the evening meal.

"I have some fresh corned beef and cabbages we can add to our stew tonight. Imagine we'll be eat-in' plenty of cured bacon and fresh quail over the next few months. Won't be long 'til we're good and sick of it all. Might be nice to have something a little different the first day of traveling. Figured we could use it all up before it goes to spoil."

Cathy's face fell, and the elderly woman looked up puzzled.

"Is everything alright, dear?"

"Oh yes, it's just, I don't eat meat, I'm sorry."

Mrs. MacGregor looked surprised for a moment, then understanding. Cathy loved animals, so she figured she didn't have the heart to eat them. Questions filled her head, but she noticed the girl didn't seem to be lacking in strength, and her complexion was glowing.

"I have an idea. How 'bout we hang two pots over the fire? I'll add the corned beef to mine. You can take more of the vegetables for your stew."

Cat sighed in relief. "I have some nice lentils and fresh herbs you can use in yours if you'd like."

"Perfect. I packed up some squash and tomatoes before we left, and of course the cabbages. They won't last long on the road, so let's share 'em tonight."

The matronly woman reminded her of her mother—her generous nature and quiet resolve was so similar. She was determined to fight no matter what and oh, how her ma fought those last few weeks. Her eyes burned as she pictured her mother's final days—twisted, flushed with fever. She bit down on her bottom lip, struggling back tears. The wagon's canopy cover was pushed to the side as she sorted through her cooking utensils and ingredients for the night's supper. She fetched her cauldron stored in the far corner, glancing toward the baby raven. One eye opened, fluttered and closed again as he nestled his beak against his chest.

Satisfied, she dragged a storage barrel to the back end of the schooner and spooned out a generous portion of lentils into a tightly woven basket. Fruits and vegetables hung in wicker netting above the barrels of grains and rainwater. She chose a plump yellow onion and a few red potatoes. A collection of herbs lined a wooden shelf near the entryway. Dried branches of sage and rosemary were placed in the basket. Once they'd finished organizing ingredients for supper, the women took their buckets to the river. As they filled their pails, the sound of children's laughter floated past. Youngsters bathed in the dark water as their mothers watched in silence. The water was quite silty, with tiny insects swirling along its surface; so, they skimmed the top, then added a few handfuls of cornstarch to sweeten the taste. They'd let it sit awhile to allow time for the silt to settle.

Mr. MacGregor, having finished preparing the cooking fire, hurried over to help the ladies carry the water back to camp. His wife tried to shoo him away, but the old man just smiled indulgently. Cathy was surprised at how strong he was for his age, carrying the buckets as if they weighed nothing. The women struggled to keep pace as he climbed the steep hill.

"I was thinkin' of hanging canvas across the wagons tonight. Wind's awful bad. Might give us a little protection and help keep the fire from going out."

"Wonderful, Mr. MacGregor. How can I help?"

"Oh, I can manage, lass." He looked relieved to have something to keep him busy.

"Perhaps you can just help the misses with supper?"

"My pleasure, sir."

He set down their buckets by the fire, then turned toward his wife, giving her a quick peck on the cheek. With a little configuring, he covered the sides of the wagons in a makeshift barrier. The canvas helped keep out some of the draft, but the icy wind still managed to sneak through.

Meanwhile, the women focused on dinner preparations. The air was growing cooler as the sun disappeared behind storm clouds. Mrs. MacGregor pulled her shawl close to her chin, her gray hair fluttering about her face. Cathy noticed the pain in her eyes and focused on making tea. Once the water was warmed, she stirred in her nettles. The hot beverage was poured into tin cups—a welcome relief to them both. They worked together in comfortable silence, cutting up fresh potatoes, cabbage, and tomatoes, placing them into the boiling pots. Lentils, flour, and barley were stirred in next, and the stew began to thicken nicely. The crisp scents of rosemary and sage filled the air as the sun set in the west.

Bullfrogs serenaded the campground with their evening harmonies, while families went about preparing their own cooking fires. Off in the distance, stray cattle were driven toward the corral; deep bellows announcing their arrival. Most went willingly enough, seeming to understand the commands of their masters. The manure stench took a little getting used to but would soon become a normal part of trail life.

As the stew thickened, her stomach grumbled in anticipation. She ladled a generous portion into a tin bowl and moved closer to the campfire. The MacGregors were waiting with their meal in hand. Following grace, they ate their supper to the steady hum of frogs and crickets. A few lonely coyotes cried out from the hillside. Their first day of travel was coming to an end.

WHEN SUPPER WAS OVER, CATHY HELPED CLEAN THE DISHES, SCRUBBING them with leftover river water and a small bar of lavender soap. Afterward she tiredly said goodnight, making her way back to her wagon, a kerosene lantern lighting the way. The little raven was sleeping peacefully in his makeshift nest. Exhausted, she moved her quilts aside her straw-filled mattress and bedded down for the night. Sleep enveloped her like an old friend.

Chapter Three

THE CRIMSON SKY DARKENED AS SHE WANDERED OVER DRY PRAIRIE GRASS, searching for something just out of reach. As the sunlight faded, a humming sound pulsed across the valley. Quickening her pace, she hurried toward a large oak tree, then came to an abrupt stop, gazing up at a knot of ropy veins quivering beneath its bark. An oily liquid flowed forth from the roots, blackening the earth as it traveled. Ash floated in the air, drifting about like sinister snowflakes. Swirls of vapor rose toward the heavens, blotting out the sun. Deep within this infinite darkness came the sound of beating wings. Ebony feathers flashed across milky white branches, inky eyes glowing in the fading light.

A warm breeze blew past, bringing with it the odor of death and decay. The aroma was putrid, and her stomach protested. The mound of earth vibrated as skeletal hands clawed their way to the surface. She watched helplessly, unable to move.

Help us. Please help us! Anguished cries traveled on the wind.

A hand settled on her shoulder. Cathy turned, her eyes widening as she studied the young man in shadow. A wolf hide was tied across his shoulders, revealing a broad chest covered in dark symbols. Ebony eyes pierced through her, seeming to study her very soul. He smiled sadly, reaching to push a lock of curls from her eyes.

"You can't outrun the inevitable, Little Raven."

Smoke filled her nose as intense pain settled in the base of her spine. In an instant, the ravens took flight, powerful wings beating about her face and body. Lightning streaked across the moonless sky. Then, there was nothing but darkness.

Chapter Four

Cʜᴀᴛʜʏ ꜱᴀᴛ ᴜᴘ ᴀꜱ ᴀ ᴛʜɪɴ ʙᴇᴀᴍ ᴏꜰ ʟɪɢʜᴛ ꜱᴛʀᴇᴀᴍᴇᴅ ᴀᴄʀᴏꜱꜱ ʜᴇʀ ᴘɪʟʟᴏᴡ. Songbirds were greeting the morning with their cheerful harmonies. As she stretched, her right hand brushed over a pile of ebony feathers, causing her to jump out of bed and check on the baby bird. She sighed in relief, seeing he was unharmed.

"So, where did these come from?" She asked, raising an ebony quill to her face.

The young raven chirped in response, his mouth opening and closing rapidly. Half-awake, she pushed the canopy curtain open to bring in some light. She prepared the bird's breakfast, dripping a rich paste into his wide beak. Satisfied, he started to preen himself, eyes focused on his new mother. Cathy reached her hand down and stroked his head. He closed his eyes to enjoy the attention.

"I guess you need a name, little one. Let me think..."

She studied her charge with amusement.

"You are a bit of a mystery...a dark beauty...perhaps we'll call you *Midnight*?"

The bird chirped in response, fluffing his feathers up like a tiny porcupine.

"Alright, my friend. Midnight it is."

She gave him one last caress before heading outside. In the cool morning light, she prepared a pot of coffee over the dying fire. She was up before the MacGregors and was grateful for a few moments to herself. Her mind kept drifting back to her strange dream and the inky feathers by her pillow. The sky began to darken as she looked to the heavens, noticing a band of storm clouds overhead—a roll of thunder echoing off in the distance.

Once she'd finished her second cup of coffee, she headed toward the riverbank. Mr. MacGregor placed a canvas barrier over a clump of birch trees the previous evening, allowing some extra privacy for the ladies. Cathy was relieved he'd come so prepared. This was one thing she didn't plan for. Cat undressed and submerged herself within the chilly currents. An overcast sky shadowed the cool water splashing around her hips, lathering up with a homemade bar of lavender soap. Chilly as it felt, it was wonderful to wash the dust from her body. A pair of bright red cardinals chirped and played in the branches above—their colorful feathers in startling contrast to the gray sky. After her bath, she joined the MacGregors as they helped themselves to fresh coffee. Mr. MacGregor doused the remaining flames from the campfire with a bucket of water before packing up his wagon. Moments later, the horn sounded, and the travelers were on the road once again.

By midday, the first drops fell. Cathy's mind wandered as the wagon bumped and swayed, the sky darkening over the long caravan. A cold shiver ran down her spine, and she pulled a knit shawl around her shoulders. From the corner of her eye, she noticed a large wagon approaching on her right. The schooner kept pace for the next several miles, but the team appeared to be struggling. One of the animals, a petite sorrel mare, displayed a noticeable limp along with a thick layer of froth around her muzzle. Saliva bubbled down her neck, dripping out foamy clots along the trail.

Cathy waved to get the driver's attention. He pulled up closer as she leaned out her wagon.

"Sir, would you like me to look at your horse on the next stop? The mare's limping quite badly, poor girl. I have some salve and bandages in my wagon."

"Mighty obliged."

Minutes later, the horn sounded signaling the caravan to pause for lunch.

Mr. MacGregor came down from his wagon and introduced himself, giving the stranger a firm handshake. Cathy noticed the way the men sized up one another, each with a guarded smile.

"I can start lunch if you want to help the poor horse," Mrs. MacGregor called down.

"Appreciate it."

Cat climbed inside the wagon to retrieve her medical supplies. She'd prepared a salve before the journey in case her mules showed any issues along the trail. The ointment was always nice to have on the farm, so she imagined traveling would be no different.

Finding what she needed, she hopped down with basket in hand and headed over to the injured mare. The horse snorted in relief as she stroked her sweaty neck. Cathy studied the leg a moment, her head cocked slightly to the side. The wound was then cleaned thoroughly and dried. One hand caressed the animal, while the other applied the ointment. The lavender scent eased the mare's nerves as she nibbled away at the edges of Cat's sunbonnet. With a strip of muslin bandage, she wrapped the leg from hoof to fetlock. A quiver ran up and down her right flank, where several flies landed, tongues darting out to lap up fresh blood. Cathy imagined the laceration was the result of a recent lash strike. She pursed her lips as she studied the animal. It pained her to know the pony was treated so carelessly.

Most seasoned farmers realized horses were not the best choice for pulling wagons over long stretches of travel. Mules and oxen were more capable, getting by on less grass and water. She glanced over at the mismatched team. The mare's partner, a young ginny mule, appeared healthy and strong in comparison. Apparently, the petite mare was unable to pull her weight. She gave the cut a few dabs of salve, wiping the remains on her cotton apron. The horse's owner stood behind, studying Cathy with an appraising look. She turned toward the man and took a step closer.

"This should help her leg a bit, but rest is what this pony needs."

"Well, sweetheart, there's no time to slow down with the caravan's schedule. I'm heading to the Sacramento River, need to make it before the cold weather sets in. Imagine I can get another horse or mule when we pass the next town. This old nag is worthless to me now, might get a dollar or two from the slaughterhouse for her if I'm lucky."

Cathy grimaced as he spoke, saddened by his complete disregard for the animal. She wanted to give him a piece of her mind but imagined the words would fall on deaf ears.

"Perhaps we can at least keep her comfortable. She's one of God's creatures, after all."

He grinned, flashing perfectly white teeth. It was a handsome face, tan and rugged—a strong jawline with a hint of afternoon shadow—pleasant to look at, and yet, there was something about his hazel eyes she didn't like, something not quite right.

"You're of course welcome to help her any way you see fit, darlin'. Appreciate it. Guess I can set pace with your wagon, seeing my horse is slowing me down anyways."

Why did he seem so strangely familiar? The answer was just out of reach…like a bad dream which dissolves upon waking. He continued talking as her mind wandered, trying to figure out where she'd seen him before.

"Did you hear what I said, darlin'?"

Cathy was shaken from her musings and looked up startled.

"I'm sorry, what did you say?"

"I was askin' your name."

She could feel the hairs rising on her neck as he stepped closer, looking down with a raised eyebrow.

"Cathy Brennan." Her mind was foggy as if waking from a dream.

"Well, it's a pleasure to meet you. The name's Jason Edwards." He took her hand firmly, raising it to his mouth. His lips brushed over, the corner of his mouth rising at the corner. She found herself unable to look away from his bright, cold eyes. Her body felt heavy, unable to free itself.

She wanted nothing to do with this man but struggled with her conscious over the mare's plight. It seemed like an eternity before he released her hand. She backed away, heading over to Mrs. MacGregor. Her body trembled as she helped prepare the bowls of beans. A few remaining chunks of tomatoes and zucchini were spooned out on top. The women offered the men their lunches before preparing their own plates.

"Mighty obliged," Jason said. He watched Cathy as she busied herself by the cooking fire.

When lunch was over, the horn sounded, and the wagon train moved westward. The travelers would not stop again until suppertime.

Her mind drifted as they drove over the vast terrain, past miles of lush prairies and forested hills. As the sun set in the west, the horn blew once again; men hollered out from one end of the train to the other, announcing was time to stop and make camp.

Scouts rode ahead on horseback, searching for a suitable campsite. They chose a spot close to the woods, intersecting a long creek bed. The clou cover was thick, blocking the setting sun lowering in the west. Red streaks crossed the sky, contrasting with the milky haze. Songbirds sang out their final harmonies as dusk settled down onto the valley.

A herd of elk appeared just outside the outskirts of the dense woods. Two young calves frolicked and played as their mothers watched in silence. The youngsters reared and kicked, prancing about on spindly legs. A twelve-prong buck surveyed the land cautiously, turning toward camp at the exact moment a sliver of light penetrated the forest canopy. Rifle fire erupted as a bullet headed his way. A blood-curdling bellow escaped its mouth; the majestic creature dropped to its knees, thrashing on the ground.

Its cries were a mixture of agony and despair. The birds in the trees took flight, their melodies silenced. Cathy gasped, covering her mouth with her hand. She observed the herd flee back into the forest, leaving their leader fighting for his life.

Meanwhile, the horses and mules, alarmed by the unexpected gunfire, reared and stomped, sending clouds of dust into the air.

Mr. MacGregor cried out, "Whoa, girls, whoa, my lovelies." He eased his team with a firm but gentle voice. His animals calmed, their attention diverted by a bucket of oats he'd placed before them. They lowered their heads, focused on dinner.

Jason jumped down from his wagon and faced his neighbors.

"Shot the buck square in the gut as he stood and breathed."

Mr. MacGregor, though a hunter himself, was visibly shaken.

"Jeezus, Mother, and Joseph! You can't be shootin' so close to the wagons, lad. Our mules went mad when they heard the shots! You spooked them terribly, and your buck's still alive. It wasn't a clean kill. Should o' shot him in the back of the shoulder—through the heart and lungs. Do you ken? Lord have mercy…"

The elderly man was red in the face, shaking his head. "Need to finish him off, son. Can't let him suffer." His mouth pinched together, and his brow knitted as he looked over at the writhing animal.

Jason's eyes narrowed as he studied Mr. MacGregor. The hunter deliberately took his time walking over to the elk. He looked back at the old man, an odd expression on his face, almost gleeful as if relishing the power of life and death. Smiling to himself, he gave one final shot to the buck's head. The animal ceased struggling, as blood pooled around its lifeless corpse. The dead eyes no longer seeing glazed over. Then there was silence.

Chapter Five

WORD SPREAD THROUGH CAMP REGARDING THE DOWNED ELK. MEN AND BOYS from neighboring wagons offered to help dress the buck in return for a share of the meat. They worked together and moved the body toward a grove of birch trees. They'd butcher it out of sight of the horses and mules, cutting much of the flesh into strips which would be salted, then hung on the wagons to be sun-dried into jerky.

Mrs. MacGregor studied the young woman, a knowing look in her eyes.

"How about we get you some tea, dear. You look white as a sheet."

Cathy nodded and climbed down from her wagon. She was grateful for the elderly woman's silence as they worked together preparing dinner, not quite ready to discuss what just happened. Mr. MacGregor fetched their largest pot from the wagon and carried it over to his wife, seeing they'd have company tonight. They worked together to hang a long metal rod over the pit, allowing space for both the stew and ribs. Once the fire was started, the women peeled and chopped onions, potatoes, and carrots, placing them into the boiling water. Cathy added dried lentils, kidney beans, barley, and flour to her pot, stirring the fragrant mixture until the broth thickened.

Mrs. MacGregor waited for the men to finish dividing up the elk meat. They'd use it sparingly over the next few days, saving much of the cured jerky for future use.

The sun was setting as their neighbors made their way toward the campfire. Jason invited the men and their families dressing the elk to join them for dinner. Cathy recognized one of the wives as the woman she'd seen by the river their first day of travel. Her pregnant belly swelled beneath a handmade shift, dark shadows under her eyes. Her name was Rachel Cohen, and she and her family were headed to the San Francisco territory. The woman's husband was offered a banking job, which she hoped would provide the means to start their lives over. Mr. Cohen's blond hair blew in the breeze, as he caressed his wife's frail shoulders, a look of concern in his aquamarine eyes. Their two children leaned against their mother with sleepy expressions on their dusty faces. The boys' hair and eyes were the same shade as their fathers.

Mrs. MacGregor walked toward the pregnant woman offering a bowl of stew. She smiled and nodded. The children helped their pa hang the rack of ribs over the fire. Cat wrinkled her nose in response to the gamey aroma. Another family soon joined them, Ned and Marjorie Johnson, along with their teenage daughter, Bella Jane. The girl's striking red hair was tied back in dainty pink ribbons. Her fair skin was a milky white contrast to her bright curls. She dressed as if ready to attend a ladies' luncheon rather than crossing the great frontier. The silk dress and lace boots seemed out of place in the crowd of travelers. Most of the women wore simple shifts or homespun dresses of gingham or calico. Cotton aprons covered their modest attire.

The girl's mother looked nothing like the daughter. Her mousy brown hair was pulled back in a tight bun, and she wore a modest frock buttoned up to the collar. She rushed back and forth, hanging on her husband's every word. Mr. Johnson was a large man in his early fifties, with a graying beard and balding head. His thinning hair was greased back in a severe comb-over, a few loose strands blowing in the wind. A sour expression remained on his face throughout suppertime. He'd look up from his meal every so often, pale, beady eyes surveying his neighbors suspiciously. His wife, having finished serving him, wrung her hands, anticipating his next order.

Once everyone was seated, Jason boasted about the adventures he planned on having once he reached the Sacramento Valley.

"There's gold nuggets the size of potatoes." He gestured with his large hands. "They're ready for the taking for those brave enough to try."

A murmuring went through the crowd as he spoke of the great fortunes just waiting to be made down by the Sacramento River and Sutter's Mill. A shorter man in his twenties made his way to the fire; a leaflet clutched in his hand.

"It's true. I'm planning on going there myself. Got this flyer, says gold is sittin' out in plain sight! You can find heaps of nuggets in the river, the hills —everywhere! Sounds like a sure thing to me."

More men came over, talking amongst themselves, taking turns reading the flyer and agreeing it was government advertised so it must be true. Several wives appeared uneasy as their husband's excitement grew. The gold fever burned bright.

❦

A GROUP OF TEENAGE BOYS PUSHED THEIR WAY THROUGH THE CROWD, THEIR eyes widening as Jason spoke of treasure-seeking and the savages he'd shoot if they dared get in his way. Bella Jane watched him spin his tall tales, all the while admiring his handsome face and bold talk. He gave her a wink, and she blushed hotly, flushing all the way to her strawberry curls.

Afterward, Jason went back to his wagon to retrieve a jug of whiskey. Several men held out tin cups, anxious to get their fill. They took turns patting him on the shoulder. Mr. MacGregor shook his head when the alcohol came his way, a brooding expression on his face.

With all eyes on him, the now-famous hunter moved over to the animal's hide. He reached toward the back and retrieved its heart, which he'd saved for last. The teenage boys whooped and hollered as he raised his trophy high in the air. The firepit stirred and crackled in the wind—shadows danced and played upon the ground, while lonely wolves howled in the distance.

Crimson droplets rolled down his hand, falling like teardrops toward the dry earth. He glanced at Cathy as she stared in horror. With his eyes locked on hers, he lifted wet fingers to his face, licking away at the sticky blood. His tongue darted over the corners of his mouth; firelight reflected in his hazel eyes.

"Darlin,' I'd be happy to share my treasure with you… seeing you helped my pony this afternoon."

She bit down on her lower lip and whispered, "No, thank you."

His eyes narrowed as he regarded her. "Your loss, darlin'."

Cathy's stomach tightened as she watched him insert the pointy end of a knife through the meaty flesh. The heart sizzled and popped as the flames touched the moist surface. A haze of smoke rose to the heavens. Clouds drifted across the moon, darkening the campground. A horned owl cried out in the night; it's mournful call lost in the wind. The hunter stared at the young woman who appeared transfixed.

Mrs. MacGregor looked over with eyes full of sympathy.

"I think I'm going to turn in early tonight and hit the feathers." She patted Cathy's shoulder, trying to distract her from the gruesome scene by the fire. "We have a long road ahead of us tomorrow."

Mr. MacGregor guided the women by their elbows, escorting them to the wagons.

The men in the group stood up to let the ladies pass, a few of the lads stealing admiring glances at Cathy. Mr. MacGregor gave the young bucks a warning look before lowering his wagon cover. The boys looked away, feigning innocence.

With a pull of the canvas, there was immediate relief from the chaos outside. Most families set up makeshift tents to hunker down for the night, sometimes even sleeping on top of blankets under the star-filled sky. There was simply not enough room inside the wagon to fit both people and supplies, but Cathy, alone in her schooner, enjoyed extra space for a mattress. She had the advantage of being off the cold ground, somewhat protected inside the canvas coverings.

Yawning, she tilted her kerosene lamp toward the baby bird. He'd eaten his fill of ground seed paste and was fast asleep. In exhausted surrender, she flung herself onto the bed, reaching for her diary underneath the pillow. The day was troubling, to say the least, so perhaps she'd make sense of it in writing.

As Cathy stared at the blank page, her mind drifted back to the downed buck and its terrible bellowing. The image sent a shiver down her spine, and she pulled the quilt over her body. She found it difficult to concentrate with all the noise outside. The men at the campfire were becoming increasingly loud as the whiskey took effect. She could hear their raucous laughter and suddenly found herself thinking of Shane.

How was his first week of traveling going? There was something comforting about his gray eyes; they reminded her of home. He was always so kind and steady, eager to help at a moment's notice. Perhaps she'd been too curt the last time they'd spoken. The loss of her mother was devastating but she was beginning to realize how she'd shut out those closest to her

Shane didn't deserve it. Maybe she could try to explain her feelings to him. He must be up tonight, guarding the camp with the other young men on duty.

Cathy moved the blankets around her body and fumbled for the Rosary stashed underneath her pillow. She recited Hail Marys and Our Fathers, pausing each time to pray for her departed loved ones and those closest to her. Her eyes became heavy as she drifted into a fitful sleep.

❧

SHANE STOOD AT THE EDGE OF CAMP, RIFLE RESTING COMFORTABLY AGAINST his right leg. His mind wandered for a moment, lost in thought. He anticipated his night shifts ending, hoping to visit Cathy in a few weeks. An orchestra of crickets serenaded the campground as his mind drifted back to his childhood friend.

He couldn't remember exactly when it happened. All he knew for certain was his heart belonged to the pretty green-eyed girl. He'd never struggled with attracting female admirers, but she was the only woman he'd ever love. His very soul yearned for her sweet smile and gentle touch. Vivid, emerald eyes made his heart ache with wanting; he'd gaze at them all day if she'd let him, but her mind was elsewhere these days. She'd never been the same since her mother's passing. He knew she felt responsible for it. There was nothing she could have done for her ma, but she didn't believe it. Cat was a fine healer—the best he'd ever seen. God knows she tried. Perhaps he could help ease her burden in some way if she'd just let him.

His daydreams were interrupted by the snapping of twigs.

"Who's there?" His question was answered by a high-pitched giggle. A dark-haired man emerged from the thicket—a young woman following close behind. The red-headed girl held tightly to the gentleman's arm, swaying as she walked. A hand-knitted shawl kept slipping down her ivory shoulders, wiry red hair covered in dry leaves and pink ribbons.

Shane studied her with a look of concern. He realized she couldn't be much older than fifteen or sixteen.

"You're not supposed to be outside the campground at night. I might o' shot you; thought you were bandits."

"Calm yourself, boy. Nothing of concern here, just taking a walk on this lovely night."

The girl giggled and swayed as the man held her firmly by the elbow.

"Your wife, sir, looks like she might be ill."

"What a funny thing to say, considering I don't have a wife." He smirked, reaching for a bag of tobacco in his back pocket. He popped a plug into his mouth, before spitting out a wad of dark juice.

The teenager started to laugh, then stopped abruptly with a hand over her mouth. Her eyes pinched together as she heaved, vomiting all over her lace boots. The man looked down at her with disgust.

Shane studied them. "Better head back the both of you before the entire camp wakes up."

⬥⬥⬥

CATHY TOSSED AND TURNED, DREAMING OF THE UNSPEAKABLE.

The village was on fire. Women grabbed their children, trying to flee into the night. A little girl waited outside a burning hut, grasping a doll made of dried leaves and maize husks. She sobbed quietly, tears trickling over the faceless toy. She waited for parents who would never return. Men and boys tried in vain to fight off the pale ones. Their well-made bows and arrows were no match for the rifle fire which mowed down entire families in their tracks. Bodies covered the hillside for over a mile in length. Buzzards circled the carnage in lazy loops, dark omens shadowing a bloody sky. A herd of buffalo thundered across the meadow, panicked by the fire igniting the dry prairie grass, their dark hides disappearing into the haze.

Anguished cries rose to the heavens, praying to the *Great Raven* to release them from their suffering.

A young woman raced along the riverbank, eyes burning from the thick smoke. She held her daughter's hand tightly as they ran, emerald eyes glowing in the haze. The mother absently pushed back a lock of ebony hair from her sweaty forehead, glancing down at the young girl.

"Not much longer, daughter. We'll be safe once we make it to the water. Perhaps we'll see father soon."

She could make out the large oak tree on the top of the hill—a thin beam of light illuminating the branches like an ominous beacon. She knew the river was close, so she quickened her step, brown moccasins padding over the dusty earth. Hearing footsteps behind her, she quickened the pace.

"Elizabeth!"

She slowed to a stop with hands resting against her hips, leaning over to catch her breath. In the moment, she forgot everything except the beauty of the young man standing before her. Raven colored hair flowed over broad shoulders and down the small of his back. His bare chest glistened with sweat, lean muscles straining as he exhaled. The aroma of fresh oak filled her senses as she gazed into his loving eyes.

"Go swiftly to the river, hide yourself in the cattails. Wait for me to return."

"Come with me, my love." She reached for him with outstretched arms.

"Ahpay!" The little girl jumped up and down, trying to get his attention. He placed his hands around her face, leaning down to plant a kiss on her freckled nose.

He smiled sadly, shaking his head, looking at his wife and daughter. "I have to go back to the village."

He pushed back a lock of ebony hair from the woman's damp forehead, gently kissing her full lips. She glanced up into almond-shaped eyes full of love and regret, then reluctantly let go of his hands. Something of a smile surfaced as he turned to walk away.

A buzzing sound filled the air as a bullet whistled past, tearing through his neck in one fatal blow. The young warrior fell to his knees, clutching his throat, blood spurting between his fingers like flowing waters. A single tear ran down his cheek as he fell toward her feet.

Grief-stricken, she threw herself across his lifeless body, keening loudly, her soul torn in two. Rough hands pulled her away from the boy, dragging her toward the great oak. She kicked and screamed, fighting with every ounce of strength. Her nails raked the stranger's face, scratching dark crimson lines over his pale skin. She flew backward, tossed into the air as if she weighed nothing. Her back hit the trunk with a dull thud. An agonizing bolt of pain jolted through her spine as she slid to the ground, unable to move.

In horror, she looked over at her daughter who was hiding behind a birch tree, emerald eyes wide and afraid. The woman whispered, *run!* The child looked back with uncertainty but reluctantly obeyed her mother's command. Little moccasins padded over the dry earth, disappearing into the heavily wooded forest.

The injured woman gasped for breath as the stranger towered over her. His mouth turned up in the corners, bright eyes glowing in the fading light.

"What's a white gal doing with a bunch of Indians?"

He looked down in disgust, spitting a wad of tobacco at her feet, absently wiping the spittle away from his auburn beard with the back of his hand.

"Well, it don't matter much. You got just what I'm yearning for tonight, girly girl. Nothing gets you in the mood like killin' a bunch of filthy savages."

His eyes resembled empty husks as he grinned. A cold shiver ran down her back as she looked up helplessly.

Death would visit her before the night's end, but not before the man's dark desires were satisfied by the green-eyed maiden.

Chapter Six

CATHY WOKE TO THE AROMA OF FRESH COFFEE. SHE STRETCHED AND yawned, groggy from her deep sleep. Her dreams were troubling, but she couldn't remember the details. It was not unusual to forget; memories were fleeting.

She put on a robe and checked on the baby bird. He was chattering away, waiting for breakfast. Once he'd eaten, she examined the wing. The surface appeared clean and dry, so she picked out a fresh dress and a towel and headed outside.

After a quick bath in the shallow river, she walked across the bank, heading over to Jason's camp to examine his horse's bandage before they left. Laughter erupted toward the front of his wagon where he held court with a group of teenage boys hanging on his every word. They grinned as Cathy approached, hats in their hands.

"I thought I might take a quick look at your mare before we're off."

Jason nodded absently, barely looking in her direction. One of the taller boys glanced up with interest as she examined the injured pony.

"May I help you, ma'am?"

"Thank you. Would you mind lifting her hoof?" She demonstrated for the teenager. He held the leg just as she showed him, watching closely as she undid the bandage.

"I'm looking for signs of infection." She gave the leg a quick sniff. "No bad odor. We'll want to keep it clean and dry for the next few days, hopefully by then she'll be feeling a bit better." Cat gave the animal a gentle pat on her shoulder.

"You're mighty good with animals, ma'am."

"Thank you. My father raised draft horses on our farm. Taught me everything he knew about them…before he passed away. Are you interested in learning?"

A smile spread over his face.

"I sure am, ma'am."

"You can call me Cathy if you'd like."

"Thank you, ma'am…um…Miss Cathy. I'm Donald Becker. You may call me Donnie if you want, my friends always do."

"Donnie, it is then. I'm planning on checking the mare's leg once a day, cleaning the wound, applying salve. I'll show you how if you're interested, it's not difficult."

"Thank you, Miss Cathy."

She studied him with a hint of amusement in her eyes, admiring the boy and his eagerness to learn.

The travelers readied themselves for another day's journey. Donnie joined his parents and introduced them to Cathy. They owned a large wagon pulled by six sturdy oxen. One very pregnant heifer was tied behind the schooner, lulling. From the look of her, she was ready to drop calf any day. The boy's mother, Simone Becker, was a French immigrant, an elegant woman with dark hair and ruby red lips. She sat up straight, head held high not a hair out of place. His father, Robert Becker, was ex-army, a giant of a man with a gentle disposition and quiet strength. They explained they were headed to Monterey, eager to start their lives over as cattle ranchers. They'd purchased several hundred head of longhorn before they left home. Eight young men were hired to bring the herd to their rancho. Cathy asked for the names of the wranglers, and her eyes widened when she realized Shane was among them. The women chatted eagerly, happy to know they would be traveling to the same destination. There was an immediate connection, so they planned to set up camp later in the evening.

The caravan continued its course along the Platte River for the next several weeks, passing miles of arid prairie land and roaming bison. The days blended together as they settled down into a comfortable routine, and the wagon train was soon working as a well-oiled machine. Cathy maintained bandaging the mare's injured leg in the evenings before supper. Jason did not exchange many words about it, just an occasional nod or smile. His entourage doubled since the day he'd shot the elk by the woods. Boys and men were eager for him to teach them everything he knew about gold prospecting.

Cathy noticed quite a few female admirers. His biggest fan, Bella Jane, made a habit of hanging about his campsite in the evenings after supper. She would follow him around like a needy puppy, desperate for any sign of attention, sometimes eyeing her suspiciously when it was time to change the mare's bandages.

She didn't think much of it, however; for the girl was young and obviously smitten. If anything, she felt a sense of pity, seeing he rarely glanced her way. Jason embellished on his gold hunting schemes, creating a buzz of excitement among the men at camp. His tales became more elaborate as the days went by, often boasting about the "redskins" he hoped to encounter, and how he'd have no qualms putting a bullet right between their beady eyes. One of his favorite stories was how his father assisted the government in taking out an Indian village back in the 30s. He appeared delighted whenever he'd describe how they'd burned it to the ground, his entourage cheering him on as he went into horrific details concerning the massacre.

Cathy was troubled by his talk. She hoped he was merely showing off for his friends and was not actually intending on hurting anyone. She couldn't understand the way people could turn so ugly when it came to the differences in race. The situation always saddened her whenever she'd come across intolerance, and she was not alone in her feelings.

Donnie would wince when he'd overhear their cruel comments and laughter. He no longer spent time with Jason and his posse, and Cathy approved. Yet, she noticed the other boys shunning him, sometimes even teasing the shy teenager because of his gentle nature. He appeared to take the bullying in stride; this was not the first time he'd been made fun of for being different.

The adolescent seemed to prefer the company of women and offered his assistance whenever he could. He soon became a regular member of Cathy's campsite along with his parents. They'd set up their tents outside their wagon each evening, planning their cooking fires together, preparing meals, and discussing experiences along the trail.

Mr. MacGregor and Robert Becker became quick friends as well. The men enjoyed hunting together in the early evenings, bringing back an occasional antelope, more often rabbits or quail.

To make the wagons light as possible, the travelers pared down their possessions, sometimes lightening their loads by ditching unnecessary items on the road. Seeing discarded furniture, clothing, even barrels of flour or grain was not uncommon. They kept their wardrobes simple, washing the same dresses, shirts, and pants repeatedly. Because of this, buttons often went missing, or there would be small tears which needed mending.

Donnie showed an interest in helping, so Cat taught him how to sew and patch. She was surprised how quickly he absorbed her teachings. Many of the ladies in camp soon envied his skilled needlework.

Unfortunately, it also became another reason to be teased by the other boys. They nicknamed him *Dainty Donald* and taunted him at every opportunity. He tried his best to ignore the jabs, but Cat knew it bothered him. Sometimes, his father would take him aside and give him words of encouragement, telling him not to let anyone ever make him doubt himself. He was fine just the way he was. Donnie would look up at his father with so much love and gratitude, causing Cat's eyes to fill with tears. She was grateful to have found such good and kind people to travel with. The friends would chat about their dreams and goals every evening over the campfire, dreaming of the day their challenging journey would end. Supplies were beginning to run low, and they planned to stock up once they reached Fort Kearny.

Cathy continued to acquire herbs and greens along the trail, rationing her grains and legumes carefully. All in all, things were going surprisingly well. The disturbing incident by the fire did not repeat itself, and the men's raucous drinking escapades were tapering off.

The week following the elk killing, the caravan arrived at the Loup and Platte River Crossing. The shallow banks surrounding the trail were thick with dangerous quicksand, making it impossible to cross safely. The two choices were to ferry across or take a much longer detour around the fork, adding more travel time to their rigid schedule. There was a vote among the men in the party, and they decided to ferry across.

Each wagon was charged three dollars for the trip, while most cattle swam alongside the vessels. Once they'd paid their dues, a group of scraggly middle-aged men loaded the nervous passengers, along with their heavy wagons and cargo, onto the ferry boats. Cathy noticed several of the ferries were in disrepair from frequent use, so she said a small prayer before getting on board. The captain was a seasoned sailor in his mid-sixties with a long grey beard that flowed over his impressive belly. He seemed more interested in watching Cathy than manning his vessel across the treacherous river. Unnerved by his unwanted attention, she looked over the side studying the swirling waters below. Her eyes widened at the sight of the cattle swimming across, amazed by their graceful buoyancy in the dark waters. Things were going smoothly until the caravan was nearly met with tragedy.

Halfway through the crossing, a young girl named Jane Bixby dangled her doll over the edge just as a blast of wind swept it into the currents below. Panicked by the loss of her favorite toy, she leaned over the side, toppling headfirst into the murky waters. Her mother's anguished cries alerted the father who jumped overboard, fishing out both daughter and doll to the relief of the family. They survived, but it demonstrated how perilous their trip could become. Cathy sighed when they reached solid ground. She was relieved, but also painfully aware this was one of many crossings they'd be having to make before their journey's end.

THE CARAVAN HEADED TOWARD FORT KEARNY WITHOUT INCIDENT, TRAVELING twenty miles a day, keeping the Sabbath as a day of rest, starting with early mass with Father Sebastian. His words were gentle and soothing, leaving the travelers with a sense of purpose and new-found energy. Cathy and her neighbors prepared a special brunch on Sunday, basking in their well-deserved leisure.

Cat reclined in her chair, considering the day's blessings. The friends she'd made on the trail were her new family, and she felt like she was part of something bigger than herself. As she reflected on the morning's homily, an unkindness of ravens landed in the trees, their inky eyes watching.

Chapter Seven

THE CARAVAN HIT THE TRAIL EARLY MONDAY MORNING, THE BRIGHT SKY AN infinite blue, not a cloud to be seen. They'd traveled over fifteen miles, intersecting several feeder trails. More wagons joined the caravan near the river at suppertime, and there were brief introductions as Sheriff Carpenter gave his instructions to the new travelers.

Cathy gazed out toward the landscape, realizing they were no longer alone; the prairie trembled as herds of bison thundered past, their dark hides shadowing the great plains. The animals were beautiful creatures, but their sudden appearance gave her a strange feeling in the pit of her stomach.

The wind whipped her hair into her eyes as the beasts raced across the blue-grass plains. When the dust settled, she noticed a group of men on horseback following close behind, leading their herd in perfect synchronicity. Four flank riders positioned themselves around the cattle, guiding them toward a deep ravine where the sage was dark and plentiful. The animals slowed to a stop and began feeding underneath the garnet sky. Cathy's eyes widened as one of the wranglers headed over, her mouth gaping open as she studied his muscular form. Without thinking about it, she ran toward the cowboy with arms outstretched.

Shane dismounted his horse, rushing over to sweep her up in his powerful embrace. She snuggled in close, breathing in the sweet aroma of sun-dried leather and aftershave. He reached down with his gloved hand, lifting her chin to get a better look at her face. His touch sent chills over her body, and she was hesitant to let him go. She studied him with a sense of wonder, hardly recognizing her old friend.

Along the trail, out in the wild country, the boy turned into a man. The corner of his mouth rose in a lopsided smile, steel-grey eyes a startling contrast against his bronze skin.

"Cat, you look great. How's travelin' been for you?"

"Pretty good." She felt her face blush hotly as he gazed down, wanting to say more but not knowing where to start. He grinned, taking her small hands in his. They heard footsteps behind them as the MacGregors approached.

"Ah, but would you look at Shane Mackenzie gone and grown into a man overnight," Mrs. MacGregor said. "Miss, do you even recognize the boy?"

Cathy blushed hotly in response.

The elderly woman gave her a wink.

"Well, son," Mr. MacGregor chimed in, "You must join us for vittles tonight. The ladies have been spoiling me with all their splendid cookin'. I should share my good fortune with you."

The women laughed as Jason Edwards headed over. Shane's smile disappeared when he noticed him.

"Well, I best set up my mules to grazing seeing I have an extra mouth to feed," Cathy said, "but first let me introduce you to our neighbor."

"Shane Mackenzie, this is Jason Edwards. I've been helping him with his injured mare," she said, pointing toward the red pony.

"Yes, we met a few weeks back." Shane said.

The men studied one another before speaking.

"Boy, aren't you supposed to be tending to the cattle? The last thing we need is a bunch of bulls stampeding through camp during supper. Bad enough we must live among all their stinkin' manure."

Jason studied Shane a moment, then spat a chunk of tobacco next to his dusty boots.

He stared back, unfazed by his rudeness. "The cattle are being tended to just fine. My shift's over for a couple of days. Some new wranglers joined up, so I have a few days off."

"That so?"

Cathy noticed the men sizing up one another.

"By the way, the name's Shane Mackenzie. Didn't get a chance to b properly introduced the other night. You remember, don't you? The evening when your lady friend was sick?"

Jason's eyes narrowed. "It's nice finding new friends on the trail. Makes travelin' a bit more pleasant. Don't you think? Why, just like Miss Cathy here," he quipped, eyeing her curves.

"The young lady has been so kind to me and my mare…so very eager to help out." A smirking grin moved over his face. "Yep, the little filly is good with horses and easy on the eyes, too."

Cathy blushed hotly as Shane glared at Jason, his mouth falling open in disbelief.

"Reckon' tonight should be the last bandage change you'll need to make, darlin'. I'm planning to go into town tomorrow to look for a buyer for the worn-out nag. Might get some pocket change trading her to the local butcher."

Cathy's forehead wrinkled as her stomach knotted.

"Oh, I see. Seems like a real shame," she said. Cat tried to keep her voice steady. "Your mare's a fine animal…hate to see her destroyed. Why she's just about healed now and has such a gentle disposition. I've grown mighty fond of her." Cathy glanced away as tears stung her eyes.

Jason studied Shane, noticing the way the boy hung on her every word, his obvious concern for the girl. He looked between the two and then turned toward Cathy.

A tight smile moved over his face as his tongue reached the bulge of tobacco protruding against his right cheek.

"Well maybe we could work something out, I suppose."

"Not sure I understand your meaning?" Cathy said.

Shane's eyebrows knotted as he studied the man.

"I've noticed you seem pretty confident by the cookin' fire. I could use some help preparing my meals along the trail. Maybe we could do some sort of a trade?"

She studied his face, trying to determine if he was serious.

"I do enjoy cooking, but you should know I don't eat meat and most definitely don't cook with it."

A hint of amusement shone in his eyes. There was also another emotion underneath. Jason was not often caught off guard. He took pride in his ability to read people, always being one step ahead, but this girl, he just couldn't figure her out. Then again, he relished a challenge. After all, game always tasted best when it put up a fight, and women were no different.

"You are…a unique one. Well, it don't matter. Guess I can always add some jerky. Maybe just focus on rustling me up some beans, cooking up those nice homemade breads and veggies, and extra greens to go along with the meals. The last thing I need is to come down with the damn scurvy."

Cathy's eyes widened.

Shane frowned.

"Watch your language around the lady."

Jason ignored him, turning his attention to the woman.

"Pardon my language, darlin'. Knew a few fellows back in my hometown who came down with the disease. They ended up having to turn back from the trail. Vegetables and fruits can be hard to come by when travelin'. Scurvy will make you real sick if you don't get enough. Such a miserable business— can turn the strongest man weak as a kitten. Got to be healthy when I get down to the Sacramento Valley. So, what do you say…sound like a suitable arrangement? Maybe you can cook for me, flavor it a bit with all those pretty herbs I see you collecting every night."

Cathy looked up startled. She was surprised he'd noticed, seeing he ignored her the last few times she'd changed the mare's bandages.

"If you could do these things, I think it would be a fair trade for the red pony."

"You mean you'd give her to me in exchange for cooking? Are you sure it's a fair enough trade? I don't want to be beholding to you." She studied his face, unable to read him.

"I'm sure, darlin'. Seems fair to me. Might have a few extra chores here and there I might need help with. No doubt we can come to a pleasant arrangement."

His eyes locked with Cathy as the corners of his mouth rose.

"What you say, boy?" He turned back to Shane, a look of satisfaction in his bright hazel eyes. "Seem fair?"

Shane's jaw clenched, as his fists tightened. He moved between them, turning to Cathy with a look of concern.

"I suppose you have a lot on your plate being a single woman on the trail. Are you sure you want to add the extra work to your burden? And it's not easy bringing horses across the plains. We'll be hitting desert before you know it and grass will be scarce."

She moved closer, placing her hand over his clenched fist.

"I'm sure it won't be too much work. Adding another pot or two to the cooking fire isn't difficult. I've already been caring for the mare for some time now, and the extra chore hasn't been much of a bother. As far as the grazing issue…well I suppose I might be able to fit a few hay bales and extra oats in the wagon, seeing it's just myself. There's also my mules to think about. Both my Molly and Gennie are getting on in years. Might be nice to have a third animal to help pull the wagon and take up some of the slack. Could be a welcome relief to them both. And she's such a darling girl! Why, it be awful nice to save her from the butcher."

Shane studied her with quiet resignation. He knew there was no use trying to talk her out of something once her mind was made up. The stranger succeeded in using Cathy's love for animals as leverage. He didn't like the situation at all, but he knew his hands were tied.

Cathy glanced back over to Jason and studied him with uncertainty. The man unsettled her. One moment he was arrogant, even a bit frightening, like the night by the fire. She could still picture his eyes as he licked away at the elk's heart, the dark blood dripping over his fingers. An icy chill ran down her back as she recalled the memory—like a strange nightmare she couldn't wake up from.

On the other hand, she realized the men were drinking. A strong whiskey can make a fool out of anyone, she supposed. Perhaps this was the case with Jason. He drank a little too much of the old orchard. Maybe he was just showing off for those boys who seemed to hang on his every word. She rolled up the sleeves of her calico dress as she considered her options, briefly noticing the scattering of freckles along her bare arms. She reckoned she'd be covered in them by the time she made it to Monterey.

Her mind drifted back to Jason. Most of the time, he seemed harmless enough. Women, both young and old, stole glances his way when they thought he wasn't looking. He was a handsome man, maybe too good looking for his own good. She exhaled, trying to decide. A little extra cooking wouldn't be too difficult. Earning her way in life was important, and this was a chance to pick up some extra work along the trail. It seemed like an easy exchange. But there was something still bothering her, and she couldn't quite put her finger on it…maybe even a bit dangerous.

"So, it's a deal then, darlin'?"

Cat looked up, startled from her musings.

"Yes, the exchange seems fair. I'd be mighty obliged to accept your offer."

He reached out his hand and took hers, raising it to his lips, lightly brushing her skin. A sense of uneasiness washed over her as the hairs rose on her arms. She hoped she hadn't made a terrible mistake. She feigned a smile and took her hand back.

"I best be getting busy with the cookin' fire seeing I have extra mouths to feed." Her voice seemed strange to her, faraway and low.

"Sounds smart, darlin'. Eager for your meal tonight." Jason gazed into her eyes, trying to read her, but was unable.

She could feel the heat rising to her face. There was a strong desire to climb back into her wagon and call it a night, but there was work to do. So, she backed away.

The group went to work preparing supper. Cathy brought out a second pot and extra ingredients. The men worked together to gather firewood, but the trees were sparse, so they substituted with bison patties. There was plenty to gather once the herds passed through camp. They were slower to burn but did the job.

Mrs. MacGregor offered to warm the jerky in her own pot. He happily accepted her offer, and retrieved some of his cured antelope meat, insisting they all share in his hunting spoils. Cathy was relieved everyone appeared to be getting along, although she noticed Shane and Mr. MacGregor rarely smiled while in Jason's presence.

Realizing Mrs. MacGregor was moving slow, Cat volunteered to finish the cleanup. She gathered up all the dishes into a basin by the fire, and Shane offered to help dry. They finished the chore under the light of the moon, working in comfortable silence. Afterward, they took a stroll through camp passing their neighbors' tents and cooking fires, smiling and nodding as they strolled by, stealing glances at one another.

"You seem different, Shane." She said, admiring his chiseled profile and lean muscles. Once they reached the top of the hill, they stopped and looked down over the endless prairie lands.

"I've thought of you often, Cat. Out on the trail…"

"Oh?"

"I know you can take care of yourself…it's just I worry sometimes."

She studied his eyes which appeared silver in the moonlight. He absently brushed back strands of blonde waves from his forehead, while offering his lopsided smile. As he reached for her hand, he leaned in for a kiss. Their lips brushed tenderly as they lost themselves in the moment. Shane pulled her close, and she breathed in his clean smell, feeling like she'd come home.

"My God, you're the most beautiful thing I've ever seen. You don't even know it. Makes you even more lovely."

She wanted this moment to last as she studied his handsome face.

"Well, it's getting cold, Cat, I better bring you back." The two lovers walked together toward the wagons. Shane helped Cathy climb inside, gazing upwards with a soft smile.

"Goodnight, darlin'."

"Goodnight."

Once inside, she hunted for her lamp and collapsed onto her bed. Her mind was racing, heart pounding as she opened her diary and began to write.

Chapter Eight

A CHILD RAN THROUGH A MOONLIT FOREST, TEARS STREAMING DOWN HER ruddy cheeks. She wanted to turn back, but she'd made a promise. Her plump little legs could scarcely take another step, but there was light in the distance, so she continued onward. The rich aroma of a cooking fire made her mouth water as she neared the campsite.

Two men in black sat together on a log, speaking in hushed voices. She watched them for several moments, shivering in the cold. Her legs were very weak, and when she found she could no longer stand, she crumpled toward the ground, landing in a pile of leaves. The rustling sound made the strangers turn toward the girl. Their eyes widened in surprise as they rose to their feet.

"Child, come closer."

The girl's emerald eyes filled with tears as they approached, fearing they'd hurt her like the pale man hurt her mother, but her legs were too tired to move, so she curled up in a tight little ball, clutching her tiny doll to her chest. Tears rolled over the thatch of black hair on its corncob head.

The younger man pushed back a lock of her ebony hair.

"There, there now child. The Good Lord sent you our way, and we'll care for you, little lamb."

The elderly man moved closer. "What's your name, angel?"

Her emerald eyes widened, focusing intently on the stranger. She squeezed her doll close to her chest for courage.

In a voice just above a whisper, she responded, "Catee…I'm Catee."

"Aww, there's a brave girl. My name's Father Sebastian, but you can just call me *Father* if it's easier. Catee? Perhaps you mean, Cathy?"

She nodded, dimples forming in the corners of her mouth.

The priest clapped his hands together. "Why it's a beautiful name, little lass. I wonder if you be named after Saint Catherine? The name means *pure one.*"

The priests studied the girl, who now sat cross-legged, methodically stroking the doll's hair. They worried she might be going into shock, noticing her dilated eyes.

"Are you hungry, Cathy? Maybe thirsty?" The younger man asked, pointing to his canteen.

"Paa?"

He looked down, not understanding. Father Sebastian stepped closer with a knowing look. "Oh, she's asking for a drink. The word *paa* is the Comanche word for *water.* The little girl is bilingual. What a clever child!"

He offered the water in a tin cup. She drank the serving down in three big gulps. With wide eyes, she gazed up plaintively.

"Oh, my poor child. Let's get you some more but drink it nice and slow this time…don't want to get a tummy ache."

She took the cup eagerly but did as he asked, a few drops spilling down her chin. Meanwhile, Father Sebastian ladled out a bowl of stew, with a hunk of bread, and brought the food to the green-eyed girl. She devoured the meal in minutes, wiping the juice from her chin with a trembling hand. He went over to the wagon and hunted around for a clean cloth and bowl.

The Father looked at the child's dusty face.

"May I?"

He washed away the dirt and dried her tears as she yawned, absently rubbing her eyes with tiny fists. Afterward, he offered his hand and led her to the wagon, where he lifted her inside and carried her over to a straw-filled mattress, laying her down carefully. He pulled a quilt over her and said a silent prayer. She was snoring before her head even touched the pillow.

The young priest fought back tears as he made his way back to the fire.

"I'll never understand how people can be so terrible to one another… fighting and killing over land and the color of one's skin. We're all God's children. Why can't they see it?"

"I wish I could answer that question, lad. But we must remember to focus on the good and not the bad. God always has a plan."

He nodded, gazing at the fire.

"Father, do you think we might take her to the convent when we get back home? Perhaps the nuns could look after her. Maybe they could even find a nice family if her parents aren't recovered?"

"Yes, I think it would be a fine idea. I'm afraid I don't have much hope in finding her mother and father, but we'll check with the sheriff to see if there's any survivors. From the look and sounds of the fire and rifle shots, I'm not too hopeful."

The men sat by the cooking fire contemplating the day's events, praying for those lost in the massacre. They didn't notice the unkindness of ravens watching them from the trees, their ebony eyes flashing in the darkness. With dawn came an eerie silence, the villagers' cries lost on the winds of the prairie.

Chapter Nine

THE CAMP WAS ALIVE WITH A SENSE OF EXCITEMENT. SEVERAL WAGONS joined the caravan the night before. Many more were on their way, trying to make it by dawn's first light. Cathy was interested in meeting the new travelers. There was word several gold prospectors were among the group. She imagined it might be interesting to learn their stories and perhaps meet some more families heading to Monterey. Cat's cheeks were flushed as she walked down toward the shallow riverbed. Marjorie Johnson and Bella Jane appeared to be having a heated exchange by the sandy shore.

"I don't care what you have to say about it! You stay away from him, or your father will have your hide!"

The girl's face went beet red as she dropped her buckets by her sides, spilling the water all over her lacy boots.

"Bella Jane! You fill those back up at once, young lady. You're not so old I can't turn you over my knee, girl!"

The teenager's mouth dropped open as she backed away, and when she believed she was at a safe enough distance from her mother; she stopped and glared, clenching her nails against her palms until she drew blood.

"I hate you! I hate every one of you!"

She turned and ran back up the hill, tears streaming down her pale face.

This was the first time she'd heard Mrs. Johnson raise her voice, and

Cathy felt a sense of pity for the mousy-looking woman. There was a sadness about her, and she imagined the mother's life hadn't been an easy one.

She regarded Marjorie with a soft smile.

"Oh, my. I'm sorry you heard our bickering. I've never been one to air out my dirty laundry in public. It's just my daughter, well she's gone boy crazy. I don't want her to get in trouble. Worry my husband might hurt her if he knew what she's been up to."

Cathy reached her hand toward the meek woman.

"I haven't formally introduced myself. I'm Cathy Brennan."

"Mighty nice to meet you, Miss Brennan. I'm Marjorie Johnson, but you can call me Marjorie if you like. Most do." She seemed relieved to have someone to talk to.

"Oh dear, have you heard the news about the arrivals?" said Marjorie.

"No, I haven't."

"Well, there were quite a few wagons met up last night around suppertime, some even later in the evening. Many of 'em are single men—most likely looking to join the miners in Sacramento and San Francisco." She looked toward the river, then glanced back nervously.

"But there were a few others," she paused, looking somewhat embarrassed. "How do I say this politely…they are not well…modest ladies if you know what I mean."

Cathy rose her eyebrow in question.

"I'm sorry? I'm not sure I follow."

"Oh, dear, well, I overheard my husband talking to one of our neighbors last night. You see, quite a few new wagons joined up from the eastern feeder trails heading to Fort Kearny along the Great Platte River Road."

"Oh, yes, I'm excited to meet them."

"Me too, but there's some wagons traveling together heading toward the San Francisco territory. And, well, some of these travelers happen to be gamblers and," she paused, her eyes widening, "there's even some ladies of ill-repute!"

"Interesting. I don't believe I've ever met a woman of ill-repute." Ca tried her best not to giggle, but she could feel the corners of her mout twitching.

Marjorie stared back in confusion, uncomprehending why the girl wasn more outraged by the news.

"Well, those kinds of people should not be traveling along wit wholesome folk like us. Can you imagine what Father Sebastian will say when he finds out?"

Cathy felt her patience ebbing as she studied Marjorie's thin face. She never had much time for small-minded people meddling in the affairs of others.

"I imagine he'd say something like, 'he who has never sinned throw the first stone.'"

Mrs. Johnson stared at Cathy like she had two heads.

"I have to finish making breakfast." The mother grimaced as she picked up the buckets and rushed back to her wagon.

Cat's curiosity was triggered, imagining what it might be like to meet a working girl. She believed everyone should be treated fairly, despite their profession or place in life. If they weren't hurting anyone, it wasn't her concern. She filled her pails and headed toward camp to start another day of traveling.

THEY RODE FOR SEVERAL HOURS, INTERSECTING THE BANK OF THE PLATTE River and Grand Island. Shane rode his appaloosa, Kelpie, alongside Cathy's wagon for the first few miles. Once the day warmed up, they walked across the prairie, giving the animals relief from their extra weight.

By late afternoon, they reached Fort Kearny. The travelers positioned their wagons just outside of the outpost. Various adobe huts and sod buildings had been constructed for the protection of pioneers passing through. Soldiers paced between the buildings, preparing for the new arrivals. Sheriff Carpenter headed over to give formal introductions and arrange housing for the night. The travelers set up their animals by the river near a patch of blue sage grass.

"Cat, I'd love to escort you to the shops. Perhaps you'd join me for dinner as well?" She smiled at the offer, then looked up thoughtfully.

"I'd love to Shane, but I better check with Jason to see about his supper first."

He looked down, taking her small hands in his.

"I'll go freshen up by the river and meet you in a bit then."

She nodded and headed over to Jason's wagon. As she approached, the sounds of muffled cries floated past.

BELLA JANE'S HANDS WERE ON HER HIPS, EYES SWOLLEN RED. SHE GLARED and pouted; rosy cheeks flushed with anger.

"You got me in a heap of trouble, Jason. Daddy will have my hide when he finds out." Her lips quivered as teardrops welled in her brown eyes. He looked down at her without a hint of sympathy.

"Looks like you've gotten yourself into trouble. Maybe you should have acted like a lady and kept your legs crossed." She stared back in shock, biting down hard on her lower lip.

"How am I supposed to know if it's even mine, girly?"

He studied her like an annoying insect. The blood drained from her face as she stared in horror. Tiny red spots speckled her cheeks, a startling contrast to her ivory skin. Without thinking about it, her hand shot out, slapping him hard across his smirking face.

"You're an absolute beast!" She moved to strike again, but he grabbed her fingers, squeezing as his eyes narrowed to slits. "Look, you little hussy, don't come around here again if you know what's good for you."

"You're hurting me!"

He released her hand just as Cathy was making her way over to his wagon. She watched as Bella Jane rushed off toward the woods—a blur of tears, lace, and ribbons.

"Is everything alright?"

"Yup." He chuckled and shook his head. "Poor girl's been trying to get my attention for a while now…figured it was about time to let her down easy. Guess she took the news kinda' hard."

"Oh, I see." Cathy did not want to pry and changed the subject.

"Glad you're here. I was meaning to talk to you." Jason said.

"Oh?"

"I'm going to purchase a mule later this evening. You can have the mare when I'm back. In fact, I'll bring her by tomorrow morning before we leave if it suits you."

"Wonderful. I was wondering if you'd be needing help with your cookin' fire tonight?"

His eyes glimmered, enjoying her obligation to him.

"Well, actually, I'm planning on eating at the fort tonight. No offense to your delicious cooking. Why don't you join me? My treat."

"Oh, it's very kind, but Shane already invited me to go shopping. I imagine we'll be dining there if you wouldn't be needing my services."

He regarded her a moment, his eyes empty and cold. He was not used to being told no.

"Suit yourself. I'm surprised the boy has two nickels to rub together, let alone enough to buy a nice meal for a lady."

She bit the corner of her lip, looking up with raised brows.

"Shane's been working very hard these last few weeks. He's making his own way."

"I bet he is, darlin'." He rolled his eyes. "I'm sure he'll be able to get you a nice can of sardines, maybe even some stale crackers at the country store if you're real lucky."

Cathy crossed her arms and looked him square in the eye.

"I'd appreciate you not being so rude when it comes to my friend. He's done nothing to you and it's not kind to speak of him so."

He chuckled to himself, shaking his head.

"Oh my, the kitty has claws. Don't get your hackles up, darlin'. I'm just having some fun."

Cat's face flushed as she felt her temper flaring.

"If you change your mind, I can take you to a nice restaurant deserving of such a pretty gal."

The man completely floored her. Was he asking her out to dinner? She found it difficult to determine if he was teasing her, or if he was serious. Either way, she wanted nothing to do with him. If it weren't for the mare, she'd turn away and never look back, but there was a helpless animal to consider. She sucked in her breath, trying her best to cool down.

"Appreciate the offer, but I've made plans as I mentioned before."

He glanced sideways, his eyes traveling over her curves, before climbing into his wagon. "Good night, kitty cat."

"Night."

She clenched her teeth as she stomped off, nails digging into her palms, heading to the wagon to freshen up. After she'd changed, she sat in front of her vanity and ran her brush through her long, dark curls. Her heart quickened in anticipation, imagining how their first date might be.

Shane was waiting by her wagon when she came out. He'd changed his clothes and freshened up by the stream. He wore a pair of tan slacks, along with a white silk shirt and gold vest. A few blond waves fell over his forehead, slightly damp from his quick wash. He started to smile and then froze when he saw Cathy's face.

"Is everything alright?"

"Yes, it's just…Jason is such an annoyance."

"Does he want you to cook for him tonight?"

"No…it's… oh, it don't matter. I'm eager to go shopping."

"Me too."

Shane's eyes sparkled with a hint of mischief as he grinned. Cathy noticed he was holding something behind his back. She glanced over his shoulder, trying to get a better look. He gave her a dramatic bow, then popped up with a bouquet of wildflowers.

"For the lady."

She giggled delightedly and took them in her arms.

"Oh, they're beautiful."

Shane watched her stroke the colorful petals, then leaned down and kissed her cheek before helping Cathy into the front rig. She held the bouquet on her lap, appreciating the bright hues.

He admired her in the afternoon sun. "That's a mighty pretty dress."

"Thank you."

She glanced down at the yellow material, her finger grazing over a section of frayed lace. The cloth faded with the frequent washes, but the dress was the fanciest one she owned and hoped her outfit would be suitable for a nice restaurant. Her ebony locks flowed underneath a matching bonnet. She was excited to visit the shops and stands and take a break from traveling.

The Fort was busy, wagons crowding the street while market vendors shouted out their wares to passersby. Modest buildings were set throughout the encampment offering both supplies and protection for the throngs of travelers journeying west. Along with several adobe and sod barracks, a mercantile store, post office, and blacksmith shop were open for business, selling high-priced merchandise and services to the weary travelers. Soldiers paced about dressed smartly in blue uniforms, several young men tipping their hats toward Cathy. She sighed, happy to be back in civilization, safe and sound under their watchful eyes. Following some exploring, a mercantile store caught her eye, so they decided to have a look inside.

The scent of freshly ground coffee greeted them as they entered, a golden bell jingling overhead to announce their arrival. She walked through the shop, admiring the various wares and displays. Porcelain teacups and pots were set up along shelves along the wall, while fresh fruits and vegetables were organized in baskets underneath. Shane walked over toward the front counter with his list of supplies, which included bags of flour, wheat, and grains, a few bales of hay, and barley. A gaunt elderly man with thick horn-rimmed spectacles took the paper and headed to the backroom.

Cathy strolled through the building, admiring some of the more fanciful items. She noticed colorful fabrics hanging across two hanging rods against the wall, so she hurried over to look. Her eyes lit up as she examined the embroidered lace but grimaced at the price tag and began to sort through the cotton and calico blends instead.

The boisterous sound of laughter made her glance up in surprise. She noticed a group of ladies making their way over, a dark-haired woman in the lead. Her scarlet frock left little to the imagination, an ample bosom swelling under a thin covering of mesh and lace. The stranger's ebony eyes flickered with curiosity, studying Cathy with an appraising look, while her entourage encircled her in a heavy cloud of perfume.

The Madame beamed. "Why look at you honey, if you aren't just a lovely thing."

"Thank you, ma'am."

"I'm Lola Vilonia. These are my girls, Darla, Dottie, Delphine, Debbie, and Diana."

Cathy looked at the young ladies in surprise, amused by their similar-sounding names. She was fascinated by the way they appeared to respond as one, yet at the same time, each girl possessed her own unique style. They came over one by one and introduced themselves.

Darla was a slip of a girl, with dark waves and soft brown eyes. She wore a rose-colored cotton shift with matching ribbons in her hair. Her petite body and quiet demeanor gave her the appearance of an older child or young teen. She was often mistaken for being much younger than her nineteen years. In contrast, Delphine, a tall, statuesque blonde, smiled with confidence, high cheekbones blending perfectly with her refined features. She spoke little English, her homeland of Denmark now a fading memory. She moved like a dancer—fluid and graceful—while batting long eyelashes over her startling baby blues.

Dottie, on the other hand, was a fiery redhead—short and stocky, with an even shorter temper. A scattering of freckles covered her face and body. She was the loudest of the group, impulsive and daring. The other girls looked up to her, often seeking her out for advice when trouble came their way, which was often. She was a natural storyteller, and her *gift of the gab* helped the ladies out of several unfortunate situations.

The last two girls, Debbie and Diana, possessed rich coffee-colored complexions, tiny waists, and shapely curves. Matching ivory bonnets capped their frizzy locks, which flowed down their slender shoulders. The girls' generous lips and wide eyes gave them both a cherubic appearance. The twins talked in the same cadence and tone, curtsying when introduced, then surrendering to a fit of giggles as they straightened back up.

"Nice to meet you. I'm Cathy…Cathy Brennan."

"You aren't by chance following the trail with Sheriff Carpenter, are you?" Lola asked with a raised brow.

"Why yes, I am."

"We just met up with your group last night. We're heading to the San Francisco territory."

Cat realized these might be the women of *ill-repute* Marjorie Johnson warned her about. She imagined how horrified her neighbor would be if she met them on the street.

"Do you sew, dearie?"

"Sew? Oh, yes. I make my own clothes. Thought I might pick up a few yards of fabric today. There's some pretty samples in the back. Afraid I don't have the budget to purchase the fancy satins and lace but could do with a bit more cotton and calico. I guess it's just as well. The trail's no place for delicate attire. My dresses are starting to fray mighty bad with all the washes."

"You can make dresses all by yourself?"

"Why yes, grew up on a farm. Did most of the mending myself especially after my ma became ill."

Lola studied her with genuine compassion.

"Sorry to hear about your ma. Life can be quite vexing at times. It's a roll of the dice, and you never know what numbers will be pointing up. Yep…jus a roll of the dice."

Cathy nodded in agreement, a silent understanding between them.

"Are you lookin' for work?"

"Work?" Her smile faded as she studied the buxom woman.

Lola appeared puzzled, then understanding, tossed her head back laughing heartily.

"Why, I think you've misunderstood me, dear! You're as innocent as a kitten and just about as cute as one, too!" She paused for a moment, studying her emerald eyes. "Ah, but you'd be the belle of the ball," she mumbled under her breath.

"No, I'm meaning I need dresses made for my girls. I'd be willing to pay you fairly if you'd be interested in the job."

Cathy released her breath, relieved she was offering seamstress work and not something scandalous.

"Why...sounds interesting. I've been thinking about opening a boutique once we arrive in Monterey. It'd be nice to earn a little money along the way."

"Sounds like we have a little entrepreneur!" The girls stared at their mistress blankly, not quite understanding what the word meant.

"I appreciate your drive, one businesswoman to another, but may I give you some advice?"

"Please."

"Don't let people tell you you can't be opening up a shop or any other kind of establishment. There will be folks along the way expecting you to stay home, raising children and waiting on a man. Well...it's all a bunch of hogwash! Why you're as fit and smart as any of 'um the way I see it. Just put your mind to it and let the dream happen. Things have a way of falling into place. Make sense?"

"Yes...I think so." She admired the Madam's spirit. Her profession was her business and figured it wasn't her place to judge.

"Good. Well, dearie, let's peek at those pretty patterns and come up with a plan."

The women sorted through the samples together. Lola was interested in bold colors, satin and velvet, with lace and sequins when possible while Cathy searched for cotton, muslin, and calico. She needed material that would hold up in the elements. The Madame's plans were a little more theatrical. While the dresses might not have a place on the trail, they would surely bring in clients once they reached San Francisco. If all went well, she'd make her cathouse the grandest and most dramatic in the territory. Cat was interested in creating something luxurious and creative.

"I might do a few sketches for you... before I start sewing."

"Sounds right smart! Could tell you had a good head on your shoulders the moment I saw you. Let's get some doodling paper and ink before we leave."

Cathy nodded, eager to try something new. The shopkeeper noticed the women and hurried over to offer his services. His eyes widened when he got a good look at Lola and her girls, turning his attention toward Cathy instead.

"May I help you, young lady. I have more materials in the back if you don't find what you're looking for."

"Well actually, we're here together."

He glanced at the Madame distastefully. Lola flashed her ebony eyes at the elderly gentleman, batting her eyelashes dramatically. "We're interested in creating some fancy dresses. We want um' covered in beads and lace. Lots of gold and silver sequins—the works! My designer here, Miss Cathy, will be creating these masterpieces. So....do you have any more beads and baubles we could add to the mix?" She reached down into her brassiere and retrieved a wad of folded bills and planked the shopkeeper.

The man eyed the money greedily as his tongue flicked over his bottom lip. His demeanor toward Lola changed abruptly as he flashed her his most becoming smile.

"Oh, why...yes of course, madam. I mean, um, let me fetch you some samples. Please wait here, ladies." He rushed off toward the back room.

The women giggled as the elderly gentleman returned with his arms full of velvet, lace, and satin. Cartons of beads and sequins were placed before them like royal offerings. Lola eyed them with an expert eye, signaling the shopkeeper which ones she wanted to purchase.

They sorted through many samples, and Lola chose a mixture of bright colors and bold patterns. Her clients' eclectic tastes demanded spirited costumes and theatrical attire. The salesman took turns carrying yards of fabric to the counter. Cathy selected some extra thread and needles, piling the supplies on top of some simple calico patterns for her own personal use, along with some sketching paper and ink.

Meanwhile, Shane was standing by the counter waiting for his order. Lola's girls encircled him, admiring his handsome features, giggling while his mouth fell open. They'd grown quite bored waiting for Lola and Cathy and found something more to their liking. Each girl took her turn flirting and teasing, trying to outdo the other while competing for his attention. His eyes darted back and forth between the young ladies, then widened when Lola and Cathy approached arm-in-arm.

The Madame flashed her winning smile as Shane removed his hat and introduced himself. The girls continued to hover, some even daring to run their fingers along his neck and massaging his broad shoulders. The young man smiled shyly, not quite sure how to handle all the female attention.

"Girls, give the poor boy some air. You're going to smother him with all your enthusiasm." She reached out her gloved hand which he took gently, trying his best to keep his eyes averted from her considerable cleavage.

Cathy felt a tinge of jealousy at the girls' flirtations, wondering if any of the ladies struck his fancy. She tried not to think much about it, turning her attention back to her supply list.

"Cat, I ordered some sacks of flour, grains, and oats. Bought some hay for your new horse. Figured I'd let you figure out the rest since you're doing most of the cooking."

"Thank you, Shane."

She looked toward the shelves loaded with canned foods and spices. Her basket was soon heaped with fresh vegetables, fruits, onions, garlic, and seasonings. A crate of lemons caught her eye. The colorful fruits gave her the strangest premonition she needed to stock up on them. Her hunches were usually right, so she purchased the entire batch. The store manager seemed surprised by her request but took the order happily. She also measured out some barley and lentil for her stews. She looked over the cans of beans and decided to add them to the order as well.

The shopkeeper ran up their items with a greedy gleam in his eyes. Cathy winced as he gave her the total. The prices were more than double than the ones back home. With trepidation, she reached into her purse and counted out her money, realizing she'd used up more than half of her savings between the ferry ride and the mercantile shop. Shane offered to help, but she said, "No, thank you. I need to do this on my own."

Once the Madame finished paying for her own order, she requested her purchases be loaded in Cathy's wagon.

"Honey, are you parked nearby?"

"Yes, just out front." Shane looked between the two women with a puzzled expression.

Cat whispered, "I'll explain it over supper."

"Happy to be doing business, dearie." Then to Cathy's amazement, she reached her gloved hand down her brassiere and pulled out another handful of bills. The shopkeeper stared openly at her ample bosom. Lola paid him no mind and kept her eyes on Cat.

"Here's a little down payment, doll, to get you started. I'll pay the rest when the sewin's finished… if it works for you, of course."

Cathy took the money in astonishment, stunned by her generosity.

"Thank you! Why it's more than fair."

"Wonderful, dear. Oh, and did I hear you mention you're going to supper?"

"Why yes," Shane said. "I'm planning on taking my lady friend for a nice meal tonight."

"Ah, well now, don't you make the most darling couple?" She took both their hands. "Yes, sir. You two are as sweet as pie. I've always been a romantic."

She sighed with a faraway look. "Well…" she paused, fixing them both with a meaningful glance and lowering her voice.

"You might try the *Golden Queen* for some real nice vittles. It's about half a mile up the road," she said, pointing with her gloved hand. "Just drive past the abandoned schooner, and then take a sharp right around the birch grove. You'll see a wooden building with a large golden sign out front. My friend's the owner. Name's Goldie Donahue. Quite the lady. Tonight's her last day dealin' at the casino. She means to travel to San Francisco just like me. I'm mighty glad to have her along. Why, she's a great gal…heart's as golden as her hair. Might drop in later there myself after I get the girls set up for the night. I imagine it will be quite the celebration."

Cathy watched the young women fawning over Shane and wondered what exactly getting *set up* entailed. She figured it might be best not to know.

"The girls clapped their hands together, rushing over to Lola's side. "We wanna come too! Aww…please, Miss Lola!"

The madam's eyes darkened, and her voice became deadly serious.

"You girls have work to do. Stop your beggin' this instant!"

They took one look at their mistress, then lowered their eyes toward the floor.

"Yes, ma'am." They answered in unison.

Lola glanced at their fallen faces then smiled softly.

"We'll see how the evening goes, girls…there might be some room to stop by after business."

The young women shrieked at the news, chattering amongst themselves like excited hens. She winked at her charges, then turned her attention back toward the young couple.

"Just tell um' *Lola sent you.* They'll treat you real fair."

They thanked her once again, then walked to the wagon with their purchases.

Chapter Ten

Fort Kearny was situated on the bank of the Platte River, near Grand Island where the river meets the shore. The fort was overwhelmed with the influx of thousands of weary pioneers requesting assistance from the soldiers, peppering them with frenzied requests for supplies and lodgings. Being a newly established outpost, the adobe-framed huts and sheds were a disappointment to the travelers who expected a more permanent structure. However, shops were open for business, although the steep prices were a shock to many, and there were essential services being offered.

Several members of the caravan were interested in the blacksmith shop. Wheels were beginning to loosen from their axles amid the arid climate. Frontiersmen waited in line hoping to have their wagons repaired before leaving the next morning. Their schooners took a beating under the merciless sun, shrinking the wooden surfaces and making it necessary to soak the wheels in the river to prevent the iron rims from falling off. Leather strips were often used as a kind of cushion. The constant dips along the trail caused damage, which required a professional's expertise.

Cathy bypassed the blacksmith shop as her wagon was holding up well since Shane's repairs before the journey. So, after purchasing provisions, the couple strolled leisurely across the grounds admiring various displays in the shopkeepers' windows. When they'd finished exploring, they headed back to the wagon and went in search of *The Golden Queen*. They followed Lola's directions and soon discovered a large wooden building overlooking a fresh running stream.

As the sun began to set, they heard laughter and music coming from the gold-painted saloon. Shane helped Cathy out of the wagon, and they sauntered over. Cigar smoke drifted pass along with the sounds of drunken antics echoing through the open windows.

Two burly men with pistols on their hips pushed the doors open with a heavy shove.

A large sign above their heads read *The Golden Queen*.

"Must be the place Lola was talking about."

Shane looked toward the doors and frowned. "I'm not sure if this is the proper place for a young lady."

"Why…it will be an adventure. Couldn't we at least peek inside?"

He smiled at Cat indulgently, secretly admiring her gumption.

"You're such an innocent little thing." The wrangler chuckled, gazing into her wide eyes, hating the thought of disappointing her. He raised an eyebrow. "There's going to be some undesirable folks in there."

"Why I'm up for some excitement. I'd like to see for myself." She looked up innocently, pupils dilating in the fading light.

He shook his head. "Cathy, you are just about the most stubborn woman I've met in my life!"

"I'll take it as a compliment."

"I'm sure you do." He was doing his best to appear serious but was having a tough time doing so. "We'll take a quick look, but if this seems dangerous or unfitting for a lady, we'll be leaving right quick. Sound fair?"

"It's a deal!"

He leaned down, kissing the tip of her freckled nose. Cat gazed up, her eyes gleaming with excitement. Shane chuckled and shook his head.

"Shall we?" His eyebrows rose as he offered his arm.

"We shall!"

He pushed the swinging doors open with his left hand and was greeted by tinny piano music and the aroma of thick cigar smoke and cheap perfume. Golden framed paintings of scantily clad women and ornate mirrors covered the cedar walls. Shane glanced down at Cathy who appeared absolutely enchanted by the place. She swayed along to the music, while an elderly man pounded away at the ivory keys of his dusty piano. Several couples waltzed by, keeping in time to the melody. Various tables hosted games of chance—

poker and blackjack being the most popular. Dining tables were set up around the periphery of the room, piled high with generous appetizers and entrees. Decanters of wine rested on several tables, along with beer, scotch and whiskey.

Cathy's mouth watered when she eyed the colorful salads, fresh breads dripping with butter, and baked potatoes soaked in sour cream. Young women waited the tables, darting backward and forward with graceful determination. Fishnet stockings covered their shapely legs, while satin shifts left little to the imagination. The reflection of an enormous crystal chandelier caught the couple's attention as it flickered diamond patterns across a large oval table. All the seats were taken, while several rowdy men elbowed their way over to get a better look at the dealer. Cat's mouth dropped open as she beheld one of the most beautiful women she'd ever seen.

Golden curls cascaded down her back like soft ocean waves. An hourglass figure was contained beautifully in a shape-hugging gown covered in crystal sequins. They sparkled with the dancing lights of the chandelier above. Cornflower blue eyes glanced casually over the cards she dealt, floating gracefully like soft butterfly wings. Every so often she'd overhear a flirtatious comment from a player as he stole admiring glances her way. Whenever it happened, she'd tilt her head back and laughed melodically, her white teeth flashing like polished pearls.

The couple figured the lovely lady was Goldie Donahue and tried their best to imagine such a glamorous woman on the trail. They couldn't.

Their attention was diverted when a voluptuous barmaid interrupted them by asking if they'd like *dinner* or *play*.

"Dinner, please," Shane said.

She gestured them to follow her to the back room.

Shane pulled out Cathy's chair before taking his own, then picked up his menu. A golden candle was set inside a crystal vase on the edge of the table. The flame flickered as they took their seats.

"Drinks?"

"Yes, please. Oh, and our friend, Lola, wanted us to tell you she sent us," Shane said.

"Marvelous. Well then, let me bring you a nice bottle of Champagne. She's a dear friend of Goldie, so you two must be very special."

The cowboy looked uncertain, wondering if he could afford Champagne on his budget. The girl put him at ease with a wink. "The meal will be on the house, dearie. Lola takes care of her people." She smiled and headed to the bartender to place their beverage order.

Moments later, a bottle of their finest Champagne was delivered. A portly gentleman waddled over with bottle in hand, presenting it first for the young man's approval. He gave a nod while the server released the cork with a loud pop. Cathy jumped at the sound, and Shane laughed as the bubbles filled their glasses.

They reached for their flutes, raising them high, eyes locked.

"I like to make a toast, darlin'. I appreciate you joining me tonight. I've missed you, Cat. Eager to see what the night has to offer."

They clinked glasses and took a sip of the fine Champagne. The bubbles tickled Cathy's nose, and she giggled in response.

Shortly afterward, their hostess returned with a small notebook in hand. The couple decided on two large salads and baked potatoes with sour cream and butter. After a quick glance at the menu, Shane asked if the bean and barley stew could be served without meat. The waitress's eyebrows rose in surprise but said she'd be happy to place their order. Cathy was touched by his thoughtfulness to order a vegetarian meal. She leaned back with a sigh, as a middle-aged couple waltzed by hand in hand, eyes locked adoringly. As Shane turned to watch the dancers, she studied his handsome profile, eyes wandering from his chiseled features to his broad shoulders and chest. She found herself imagining what his muscles might feel like pressed against her body, her cheeks flushing at the idea. As her mind drifted along to the melodic piano music, Shane stood up from his seat, gazing down in anticipation.

"May I have this dance?"

"Yes, thank you."

He took her hand and led her out to the dance floor. As they waltzed, their bodies synchronized perfectly with each step. Cat felt his firm body melding against hers and yearned for more. Brushing ever so lightly over her ebony locks, his fingers moving through the silky strands with delicate ease. The lamplight flickered golden highlights over the dancers as he reached up and caressed her face with the back of his hand, leaning in for a kiss just as the tune came to an end. His lips were warm and gentle, and she felt herself drifting far away.

Her head was spinning by the time he'd escorted her to their table Dinner was waiting, and their glasses were sparkling with fresh Champagne.

Shane pulled out Cat's seat, and they enjoyed their meal while discussing their plans for Monterey.

⚜

GOLDIE DONAHUE APPROACHED THEIR TABLE JUST AS THEY WERE FINISHING up with supper.

"Well, you two lovebirds must be Lola's friends."

The couple introduced themselves and thanked her for the hospitality.

"Yes, this is a fine establishment, I'll miss the place dearly, but it will be exciting to travel to San Francisco. Yep, I hear the gold's just flowing into town, and I plan to set up a brand-new saloon where the miners can spend it." Pearly white teeth reflected the candlelight as she grinned.

"Will you be joining the wagon train soon?" Cat asked.

"Tomorrow morning, I imagine. Will travel with Lola and her girls. Plan to set camp together."

"Gets a bit tiring passing all the endless prairie land, but it's an adventure all the same," Cat said.

"I imagine so. Well, I best be getting' back to my cards, darlings. Happy to be traveling with you fine folks."

"Yes, we're so happy you're joining us! Thanks again for the delicious supper and Champagne. This was a real nice treat after traveling so long."

"My pleasure."

Her shapely hips swayed to the music as she walked away, earning several admiring glances from the men in the room.

⚜

WHEN DINNER WAS FINISHED, THE COUPLE HEADED TO THE WAGON, SHIVERING in the chilly night air. Cathy excused herself for a moment to check on Midnight. A fledgling now, his small wooden bowl was replaced by a larger wicker basket. His wing appeared healthy, so the bandage was ready to come off any day. She was happy he'd healed so well but saddened by the thought of saying goodbye. She understood it wouldn't be fair to keep him once the wing mended. Shaking her head, she turned away.

"How's your little charge?"

"Looking well. Might take the bandage off tomorrow."

65

"Great news."

Shane studied her a moment, touched by her tenderness. With a gentle flick of the line, the couple was on their way. A cool breeze blew Cathy's hair into her eyes, while gooseflesh rose along her arms and legs as she pulled a shawl over her shoulders.

"Cold?"

"A little."

He reached for her tiny waist, moving closer. She leaned her head against his broad shoulder, snuggling in contently.

"Feels like a storm's a brewin'."

"Surely does."

THE RAIN BEGAN TO FALL JUST AS THEY WERE PULLING UP TO CAMP. THEY worked together settling the mules under the protection of a makeshift canvas cover. Once in place, they rushed back to Cathy's wagon. Shane helped her climb inside, grinning up as large raindrops pelted his face.

"You'll get drenched in the storm. Why don't you take shelter in my wagon until it passes?"

He nodded while climbing inside. Cathy lit a kerosene lamp, and the shadows receded to the far corners of the room. She sorted through her hope chest and retrieved a thick cotton towel, noticing how his silk shirt was completely soaked through, the damp cloth clinging to his muscular chest.

"You must be mighty cold. Here, let me hang your shirt on the clothesline."

She turned her back while he undressed, then handed him the towel without looking up. He reached for her hand instead, his gentle touch stirring her imagination. She turned to face him, and her eyes widened at the sight of his chiseled physique. Her childhood friend, no longer the innocent boy she remembered, appeared statuesque in the dim light. Somewhere along the trail, he'd become a man in both appearance and confidence.

HIS SKIN TURNED A GOLDEN BROWN FROM WORKING LONG HOURS ON TH cattle drive, while his abdomen developed into a well-defined V-shape

66

which continued down toward the waist of his trousers. Droplets of water clung to bronze skin, dripping to the floor in tiny puddles. Her pulse quickened at she studied him, and she reached tentatively with towel in hand, drying the water from his bare chest. She gazed in wonder, her emerald eyes glowing in the soft lamplight.

With the back of his hand, he caressed her cheek.

"You're the most beautiful woman I've ever seen, Cat. I've loved you for a very long time."

Cathy stepped closer, grazing his skin with her fingertips, heart thrumming in anticipation.

"I love you too, Shane. I always have…guess I was afraid to admit it to myself."

The corners of his mouth pulled up as he moved her petite body against his own. She melted toward him, delicate hands exploring taught muscles. Steel-grey eyes so full of need, he wanted her badly but wondered if she felt the same.

Shy kisses became more urgent as his fingers caressed the hollow of her neck, moving toward the buttons of her dress. Taking his time, he released each one, exposing delicate flesh. His lips grazed over her breasts as she shivered in the shadows. Outside, a bolt of lightning dashed across the starless sky, followed by a roll of thunder in the distance. The wind moaned and shook the wagon's canopy in fierce gusts.

Cathy hardly noticed the raging storm. She was enraptured by Shane's touch, and time stood still. The lantern flickered, casting soft beams across their faces, eyes burning with passion like fire behind glass. She felt his hands undressing her, fingers grazing over the contours of her skin. A scattering of goosebumps surfaced as the cold wind made its way into the open spaces of the schooner. He kissed the bumps ever so softly, lips warming the delicate mounds of her breasts, tongue flicking over nipples hardening at his touch. She let out a soft moan, running her fingers through his wavy hair, pulling him closer.

He smiled at her eagerness and placed his hand under the small of her back, lowering her down across the straw-filled mattress. Cat's body was now throbbing for him with an urgent need, and she tilted her hips against the impressive bulge in his trousers. She'd never yearned for anything as she did in this moment and was quite ready to be indulged. Shane intended to satisfy her every need and looked forward to taking his time doing so. His hand reached down, caressing her inner thigh, now just inches from her aching desire. He hesitated, looking longingly into her emerald eyes.

"Cat, are you sure?" he asked in a husky voice.

She whispered, *Yes*. He grinned down at her, falling in love all over again until the sound of anguished screams startled them back to reality.

⚜

SHANE SAT BOLT UPRIGHT, EYES DARTING TOWARD THE OPEN FLAP OF THE canopy.

"Did you hear that?"

She sat up slowly, her head still swimming from their passionate exchange.

"What was it?"

A second scream followed, along with blood-curdling sobs. Their eyes widened as they stared at one another in dazed confusion.

"What in God's name?"

"Not sure, but I better go check it out. You wait here, might not be safe."

"I'm going too."

"Promise you'll stay behind me. I'm bringing my rifle."

Wrapping her shawl absently around her shoulders, she climbed out from the wagon.

⚜

THEY WERE MET WITH CHAOS OUTSIDE. THE RAIN WAS COMING DOWN IN sideways torrents, a gusty blast pushing them backward as they tried to make their way across camp. Several tents pulled free from the mud and were sent bouncing across the hillside while their owners rushed after them in a panic. Cathy wiped at her face as the icy wind stung her eyes, making it difficult to see. Puddles were filling up the creviced patches along the blue sage grass. Muddy water splashed against their legs with every step, as hail pelted down from the heavens, blinding them as they neared the wailing sounds. Shane held up the lantern to light their way, following the cries which led them to the edge of camp.

A group of travelers encircled a large oak tree, mouths open wide focused on the screaming woman. Children held on to their parents' hands

68

absently rubbing their eyes with tiny fists. Most of the witnesses were jarred from their beds, dazed and confused.

At the base of the great oak kneeled Marjorie Johnson, hands reaching toward the starless sky, head rolling backward as she keened wildly. A flash of lightning streaked across the heavens illuminating the young lady hanging from its branches. Bright red curls blew chaotically across her milky white face. Lacy boots hung loosely beneath her, swaying from side to side in the biting wind. Another flash of lightning exposed dozens of ravens perched in the gnarled branches, inky eyes glowing under the light of the crimson moon.

Cathy gasped with her hands over her face. Shane made the sign of the cross, then pulled her close, kissing the top of her head as she sobbed against his chest. The cries of the mother rang out over the thunder, bringing the rest of the camp to bear witness to her tragedy.

Chapter Eleven

THE NEXT MORNING WAS COLD AND WET, AN EERIE SILENCE HOVERING OVER the valley. Father Sebastian sat with the grieving parents, giving council and words of comfort. The Johnson's stared blankly ahead, scarcely hearing him in their shock and confusion.

Neighbors gathered wooden storage bins from their wagons, breaking them down to make a coffin, while friends of the family prepared the ground for burial. They marked the site with a cross with the words *Bella Jane* etched into the wood. A handful of ravens encircled the upturned earth, dark sentinels in the heavy mist. Gossip spread like wildfire as the travelers debated the reasons why a young woman would take her own life.

Shane and Mr. MacGregor sat by the cooking fire, sipping hot coffee and reflecting on the night's events. Meanwhile, Mrs. MacGregor was preparing a casserole in her Dutch oven. She'd offer it to the grieving parents later in the day. Simone Becker and Elizabeth Cohen prepared their own special dishes for the family. Cat heated a second pot of coffee over the fire as Donald prepared breakfast. They worked in silence, saddened by the loss of someone so young. Jason joined the group just as the food was being served, sniffing the air and grinning.

"Smells delicious, darlin'." He glanced over in Cathy's direction. She handed him a bowl of potatoes and vegetables, while Simone added a spoonful of meaty stew from her own pot.

"Thank you, ladies."

He sat down next to the men. Jason stretched, leaning back in his chair, legs wide apart.

"Shame we'll be leaving so late today. I imagine the funeral will be a long and heavy affair. This is going to put us at least a day behind schedule. Bad enough the caravan doesn't move on Sundays. That's two days of traveling lost this week."

The men studied him with disbelief, angered by his callousness. Cathy noticed Shane's troubled expression, wondering what he was thinking.

"Hey, did you get a chance to see my new ginny?" Jason asked, oblivious to the mood of his neighbors. Cathy turned and gasped as she eyed a black mule tied beneath the tree Bella Jane was found hanging the night before. Ravens clung to the milky-white branches, casting ominous shadows across the ground.

Cathy shuddered. How could he be so insensitive? She was starting to feel trapped within a nightmare she couldn't wake up from.

"My mare's all yours, darlin'. Here, I'll go fetch her for you." He spooned up the last few bites of stew from his plate before leaving.

A few moments later he came back with the mare in tow. Cathy stared in horror, noticing several dainty pink ribbons tied into the pony's mane. Her veins felt like they were engorged with ice water. She stared at Jason, her heart racing.

"Where did you find those?" Her eyes teared as she studied the pink cloth. She reached toward the horse, caressing the silky material between her fingers. A shiver ran down her spine as she touched the velvet ties.

"Oh…bought them at the fort last night…yup…at the mercantile store Thought you'd think they'd be pretty on your new filly. Don't you like 'em?"

He shifted his feet, then absently spat a hunk of wet tobacco on the ground.

Cathy let out her breath, trying her best to make sense of things. *My imagination is getting the best of me.* She took the reins and said, "Mighty obliged."

Surly those ribbons didn't belong to the poor girl. This had to be some terrible coincidence. Her hands were shaking as she led the mare to the river to join her mules. The animals regarded one another, whinnied and hawed then dropped their muzzles to graze.

By noon, the travelers were gathered at the top of the bank by the bluegrass meadow.

The Johnson's stood next to Father Sebastian. Marjorie sobbed silently into her handkerchief, while her husband stared off into the distance, his face a mixture of sorrow and disbelief. There was a large gathering, and many tears were shed. By the end of his service, Cathy noticed several new faces joined the group. Lola and her ladies along with Goldie Donahue gathered in the back, somberly studying the grave. The women wore black dresses, quite subdued compared to the night before, but still succeeded in causing a nervous discord among the mourners. Several housewives whispered to one another behind gloved hands. Cathy hoped her new friends hadn't noticed.

Father Sebastian read from his Bible in a clear and steady voice. He ended the sermon with the following passage from Isaiah.

On this mountain the Lord of hosts
will provide for all peoples
A feast of rich food and choice wines,
juicy rich food and pure choice wines.
On this mountain he will destroy
the veil that veils all peoples,
The web that is woven over all nations;
he will destroy death forever.
The Lord God will wipe away
the tears from all faces;
The reproach of his people he will remove
from the whole earth; for the Lord has spoken.
On that day it will be said:
"Behold our God, to whom we looked to save us!
This is the Lord for whom we looked;
let us rejoice and be glad that he has saved us!"

Afterward, men and women approached the grieving parents, giving their condolences and offering service. Shane took Cathy's hand. She studied his face, wondering what he was thinking.

"Is something bothering you?"

He looked down. "Would you take a walk with me?"

"Of course."

They made their way toward the babbling creek and sat down on a large boulder by the water. Shane studied the bluebells growing along the shore. Cathy waited patiently as he gathered his thoughts.

"Several weeks back, I was posted to guard duty. I believe it was near midnight when I heard a rustling coming from the woods. I called out just as a couple was emerging from the thicket. Cat, I saw Jason...with Bella Jane."

Cathy gasped as a gnawing sensation settled in the pit of her stomach.

"They both appeared to be drinking, their clothes and hair were disheveled. Pretty obvious they were doing more than taking a walk in the woods."

He nibbled on his bottom lip, looking toward the meadow.

"Well, anyways, I asked him if his wife was sick. He made a point of sayin' she was not his wife. Jason seemed awful proud of his conquest—smirking at her like she was a trophy. A few moments later, Bella Jane vomited all over herself. Poor girl was so ill...could barely walk. She'd drank way too much. The two were having quite the spree. Well, after she'd gotten sick, he grabbed her hand and headed toward camp. Was the last I saw of them until, of course, the other night. The situation was troubling seeing the girl was so young and all. I didn't tell anyone about it though, figured this wasn't my place...but now...I just can't help wonder if maybe I'd said something to someone...perhaps this wouldn't happen like it did." His eyes filled with tears as he looked away.

Cathy took his hands in hers. "How could you have known? This isn't your fault, Shane. What happened was just a tragedy, but I understand how you feel." Now it was her turn to look ashamed.

"I was down by the creek last week when I overheard Mrs. Johnson arguing with her daughter. The poor girl ran off into the woods crying. When she left, her mother mentioned she was smitten, and worried Bella Jane would get herself into trouble. Before we went shopping last night, I saw her talking with Mr. Edwards. Didn't hear what they were saying but realized the two were having an argument. Jason didn't appear troubled by the situation, just explained how the girl was infatuated with him. He said he'd no choice but to let her down easy. Maybe I should have said something to Mrs. Johnson...gets me to wondering..."

"Wondering what?'

"Well...after hearing what you said about them in the trees together drinking and all. Could she have gotten herself with child? Was she out of options? Especially the way Jason wanted nothing to do with her."

"I don't know Cat, but this is troubling. There's something not quite right with Jason. Did you notice how he didn't even seem bothered by what happened to Bella Jane? He was more concerned with getting behind schedule than anything else."

"I noticed…and then there's the ribbons."

"What ribbons?"

"This is probably nothing…just a terrible coincidence. The mare's bows look just like the ones the girl used to wear. Startled me awfully bad…you don't suppose…"

He considered her face, absently pushing a lock of blonde hair from his forehead. "I want you to stay away from him. I'm back to guard duty on Monday, and it might be another couple of weeks before I see you again."

"I'll be alright."

"Promise you'll let Mr. MacGregor know if the man bothers you in any way."

"I promise."

He looked back toward camp, wringing his hands.

"Is something else bothering you?" Cat asked.

Shane closed his eyes and pursed his lips.

"Last night…"

Cathy glanced up startled as her stomach tightened. *Perhaps he regretted what happened.* He moved closer and took her hands.

"I've loved you for such a long time. Last night was so beautiful, and I hate to think what might have happened if we hadn't stopped."

"Oh?" Her eyes filled with tears as she looked away.

He studied her with a look of confusion, then in understanding.

"Oh no, sweetheart…you've misunderstood me! I want to be with you more than anything…you have no idea. But, darlin', I want so much more. You're my heart and soul."

His eyes were so full of sorrow; she wanted to hold him and kiss his pain away.

"I have some big plans for us, Cat. Should have some money saved up once we get to Monterey…and I forgot to tell you…The Becker's offered me a wrangling position on their new rancho. Say they like my work and seem awful fond of you, too."

Cathy's eyes glistened as he took her hands. "I'm proud of you. They're a wonderful family. I've gotten to know Simone and her son quite well. Donnie's been helping me with the mare and has quite the way with animals."

"Happy to hear it. Seems like everything is falling into place."

"Yes, and I've been thinking about starting a little business."

"Oh?"

"You know something?"

"What, darlin'?"

"Lola inspired me last night."

His eyes widening when she mentioned the Madame. "How so?"

Cat put her hands to her mouth and giggled, shaking her head. "I meant the dresses. She's paying me quite generously for my sewing. So, you see…I was thinking about opening a clothing boutique."

"What a relief!" A flicker of amusement shone in his cool grey eyes. "It's a beautiful idea. I think you'd make a wonderful business owner. Why…I bet the two of us could make a difference in Monterey."

"But, there's one question still needs answering."

She raised her eyebrows, "What question?"

He reached into his trouser pocket and retrieved a green velvet case. Inside was an emerald and diamond ring glittering in the afternoon sun. Shane lowered himself down on one knee, gazing up in anticipation.

"Would you do me the honor of becoming my bride?"

Cat's eyes filled with tears as she gazed at the sparkling jewels. "Your mother's wedding ring. I remember this growing up. So…lovely." She gasped choking back tears, her mouth trembling.

"My ma always thought mighty highly of you. Considered you like a daughter. Bet she's smiling down from heaven right now. So, what you say, beautiful? Would you do me the honor of marrying me?"

છ⊱ે

HER HEART WAS SO FULL OF LOVE SHE FELT SHE'D BURST. CATHY GAZED IN awe, heart thrumming with excitement. He held his breath, waiting for an answer.

"Oh yes, Shane!"

A smile lit up his face as he gathered her close, kissing passionately by the flowing waters. They spent the rest of the afternoon entangled in each other's arms. Once Venus made her appearance in the hazy sky, the two lovers walked back to the wagons together. Mrs. MacGregor's eyes widened when she noticed the engagement ring.

"Darlin' girl! Mr. MacGregor come and see!"

He hurried over, setting his water buckets down by his muddy boots. The elderly man studied the bright gems, stroking a clump of white stubble on his chin before speaking. He turned to Shane, patting him on the shoulder. "Good job, lad. You make a fine couple."

Cathy couldn't stop smiling while she prepared supper. Mrs. MacGregor beamed at the bride-to-be, overjoyed to see her excitement. Jason was elsewhere that evening, and his absence was a relief to both Cat and her friends. The young lovers enjoyed a quiet meal in peace, exchanging secret glances throughout supper. She found it difficult to say goodnight as her fiancé stood gazing up toward the wagon. She yearned for him to join her, but they'd agreed to wait until after the wedding. A smile moved over her face as she snuggled against her pillow, eventually surrendering to peaceful dreams.

Chapter Twelve

THE NIGHT WAS EXCEPTIONALLY COLD WITH A BITING WIND WHICH MADE ITS way through the open spaces of the schooner. Cat woke up several times, shivering under the quilts. It was close to dawn when she heard a rustling coming from the wagon cover. Believing it to be just a breeze, she closed her eyes until she felt the gentle kisses on her neck.

"Mornin', Mrs. Mackenzie."

She grinned, rubbing the sleep from her eyes. "Morning, Mr. Mackenzie."

He stroked her cheek, planting another kiss on the warm skin. She sat up in bed, wrapping her arms around Shane's tan neck, breathing in his clean scent. He hugged her for several moments before speaking.

"I wanted to see you before I left this morning. Plan to join the scouting party in about an hour. We'll be riding on ahead to check for camping sites. Have extra guard duty shifts for the next few weeks, too. Might be awhile before I can spend time with you again."

"I miss you already, my love." Cat purred against his ear, her stomach tightening with the idea of him leaving so soon.

"I spoke to Mr. MacGregor last night and asked him to keep an extra eye out. We both agree Jason could be dangerous. You just go and stop by their wagon if you have any trouble. Promise?"

"I promise." She sat up, stifling a yawn."

"Good girl." His white teeth flashed in the shadows. "I love you so much…can't stand the thought of anything happening to you. You're my life now."

"I love you. Promise me you'll be safe." She gazed into his loving eyes.

"I promise, darlin'. I'll be missing you while away, but also excited to be working toward our future."

"Me too. I'm sewin' the dresses tonight. Plan to meet up with Lola and the girls for their measurements."

"Sounds like we'll both be pretty busy."

Cathy sighed, snuggling close to his warm body. They held each other in comfortable silence until the couple reluctantly said their goodbyes. Cat stayed under the covers awhile longer, dreaming of their bright future. At dawn's first light, she climbed out of bed to check on Midnight the Raven.

"Good morning, little one."

The bird blinked in response.

"I believe today is the day to test your wings."

She petted him on the head while he preened. He closed his onyx eyes as she stroked him. She removed the remaining bandage and examined the ebony wing underneath. The broken bone mended nicely, no longer crooked and bent. He ruffled his feathers and stretched. Cat put her arm out, and he hopped up cocking his head slightly, looking out toward the rosy sky. They sat together for some time under the awning, enjoying the peace of the lingering dawn.

"You're free, Midnight, go on and fly." He concentrated on her face, seeming to understand, then flapped his wings several times as if testing them out. Satisfied, he took to the sky, a black silhouette in a sea of amber.

Tears streamed down her face as he disappeared into the morning mist. She'd grown quite fond of her little friend and would miss him.

Gathering up a faded pink dress along with her towel and soap, she headed to the creek bed undressing behind the canvas barrier. A few minutes in the shallow currents, Cathy began to feel uneasy. She waded toward the shore, alarmed by the noise of snapping twigs. Her heart racing, she grabbed her towel, dried off and dressed. The fluttering of wings sounded above as Midnight landed on the branch of a willow tree.

She stared at him, unbelieving. "Back so soon?"

The majestic bird cawed, then flew over, landing on her right shoulder.

She released a delighted laugh and stroked the glossy feathers on his head. Together they moved past the riverbank over toward the trailhead. After a few steps, she noticed several large footprints sunken in the sandy soil. Her stomach felt heavy as if she'd swallowed lead. She stared at Midnight, her eyes widening with concern. "Do you suppose the tracks were there earlier…maybe someone already bathed in the creek?"

When she leaned down on her haunches to get a better look, a colorful object caught her eyes. Her fingers reached out tentatively, grazing over the velvet ribbon. Holding the cloth up to the light, her breath hitched, realizing it was a bright pink bow.

A feeling of dread washed over her as she headed toward the wagon. She tried her best to push the anxious thoughts from her mind, but an ominous feeling stayed with her throughout the day.

THE PRAIRIE LANDS STRETCHED OUT ENDLESSLY AS THEY DREW CLOSER TO the Wyoming territory. An unpleasant aroma hung in the air by the swamplands, the uneven landscape making it difficult for travel. The caravan stopped several times as schooners became lodged within the mud. Boards were needed to help pull the wheels free from the sticky earth. The treacherous road evened out toward the afternoon. Yet, their relief did not last long as they came to another fork in the trail. So, with trepidation, they prepared themselves for a second river crossing, moving past the South Platte River over to the North Platte River along a bend known as Lower California Crossing. Once again, they paid an expensive toll and readied themselves for the dangerous trip. This time, the caravan made it across without any mishaps, much to the relief of the weary travelers.

Shortly afterward, they met another obstacle as they were forced to travel up the steep and treacherous California Hill. Cathy held her breath during parts of the journey, imagining herself rolling back down if her animals faltered. Thankfully, they managed to pull their weight, making it to the top without incident. The group took a break, enjoying the fresh air. Following lunch, they faced the task of descending Windglass Hill.

The task was not easy, as they were forced to break into groups, one driving the wagon while others held ropes to steady the schooner from the sharp decline down the plateau. Goldie and Lola worked alongside Cathy and the MacGregors. Simone's husband helped guide their way. With much configuring, the friends were successful in bringing their animals and wagons down the steep hill. Others were not so fortunate.

Two wagons tipped over halfway down, spilling out precious rations and supplies as their ropes unraveled, and the schooners pitched to their sides. Luckily, no one was injured in the accidents, and the travelers worked together to pull the wagons upright and gather up the remaining possessions.

At the end of the harrowing ordeal, they were rewarded by arriving at Ash Hollow on the North Platte River where picturesque springs awaited.

Cathy marveled at the cool, flowing waters reflecting the blue sky above. Mr. MacGregor helped her carry a barrel's worth of fresh water. Vibrant rose bushes covered the pristine oasis, as well as plentiful grasses for the hungry livestock. Cat collected a basket's worth of rose hips, then ground them down with her pestle to use for tea later in the evening.

The travelers set up camp by the glade, basking in the peace of the picturesque landscape. They fell asleep next to the cool spring, exhausted but happy they'd overcome yet another challenge along the trail.

Chapter Thirteen

SHORTLY AFTER LEAVING ASH HOLLOW, THE TRAIL FLATTENED OUT TO WIDE-open prairie lands. The monotony of the unchanging landscape weighed heavily on the travelers. So, it was a great surprise when the scenery changed one afternoon.

Cathy blinked as they descended a steep ravine, not quite believing what she was seeing. A large outcropping of stone surfaced in the hazy distance. As the miles stretched onward, she realized there were two boulder-like structures. Around noon, the caravan stopped for lunch, and they discussed the mysterious formations. Sheriff Carpenter visited their camp later in the day, explaining they were remnants of an ancient plateau intersecting the North Platte River. The formations were said to be four thousand feet above sea level. Their impressive size impressed the travelers who nicknamed the largest one *Jail*. The smaller of the two became known as *The Courthouse*.

It took three more days of travel before reaching the impressive curiosities. The caravan camped in the shadow of the mysterious stones, while children attempted to climb the rocks under the watchful eyes of their parents.

Following supper, Lola and the girls visited Cathy's campsite. She introduced them to the MacGregors and the Beckers, their eyes widening in surprise as the girls giggled and curtsied. While their friends were getting acquainted, Cat led Lola inside her wagon, lighting a kerosene lamp to illuminate the dim space.

"Why aren't you the clever one?" Lola beamed. "Look how neat and organized you are! Love how you hung your herbs in baskets."

"Thank you. Makes it easier. I've been working on some drawings I'd like you to look at. Did you happen to get the girls' measurements?"

"I did." She reached toward her bosom to retrieve the paper.

"Perfect."

Cathy thumbed through her notebook, turning to a finished sketching.

"I'd like each girl to have their own color and style. So, I've chosen a soft rose fabric for Darla, figured the hue would look nice with her dark hair and eyes. A bib of white lace will fringe the front of the gown." She pointed toward the material. "Figured it might be pretty to add some pearly beads to the waist and along the hem, a few rhinestones at the collar."

The Madame nodded in approval, as her eyes widened, noticing Cathy's engagement ring.

"Oh, dear!"

"Shane proposed the other day, and I said, *yes*."

"I'm awfully happy for you." She gazed at the jewels. "You two are as cute as can be. What does your fiancé think about your boutique idea?"

"He's real excited about my plan. Told me I'd make a wonderful business owner."

"Imagine…why you have a rare man, honey. Most are intimidated by a woman making her own way. Good for you! Well, I guess we should check with Darla to see if she likes the dress pattern."

◌✺◌

OUTSIDE, DOTTIE WAS KEEPING MR. MACGREGOR COMPANY BY THE FIRE listening to him embellish on his early days in Scotland. The fiery redhead laughed heartily, enjoying his rowdy tales. Mrs. MacGregor shook her head amused by the girl's enthusiasm. Darla offered to help the elderly woman chop vegetables, and they chatted away as they worked. Meanwhile, the twins were keeping Simone entertained, hanging on every word as she described her younger days in France.

Donald sat next to graceful Delphine while she studied his needlework with fascination. The golden-haired beauty was impressed, complimenting his form with genuine interest. He smiled, handing her a piece of fabric, demonstrating how to embroider. Her baby-blue eyes lit up once she started to get the hang of it. Donnie patiently explained his technique, and her confidence grew with each delicate stitch.

Cat was more than relieved to see everyone getting along so well. "Darla, why don't you come on in the wagon and look at the patterns," Lola said.

The waif-like girl climbed inside, her eyes widening as she studied the colorful fabric and detailed etchings.

"Oh my, Miss Cathy. This is much too dear. Why the gown should belong to a lady."

"You are a lady."

Her eyes welled up with tears.

"Thank you kindly."

Noticing Cathy's engagement ring, she let out a sigh. "Oh, it's so beautiful. I know it's a silly notion, but sometimes I dream of gettin' hitched."

"Not silly at all. I don't see any reason why you couldn't."

"Thank you, ma'am. You know, I've heard there's plenty of miners in San Francisco desperate for wives. We're going to outnumber um' when we arrive. So many single men all alone with their heaps of gold. Can you imagine? I just wonder…maybe there's someone out there for me?"

Cathy considered her big brown eyes and smiled.

"You deserve a happy life. Don't let anyone tell you otherwise."

"I guess it won't hurt to dream."

⁂

ONCE SUPPER WAS OVER, CATHY LIT HER LANTERN AND ORGANIZED HER patterns and cloth. She unleashed her creativity with each stitch, dreaming of the day she'd open her own boutique. For the next several weeks she worked on the gowns, the girls stopping by for fittings before their nightly escapades. Rumors began swirling around camp suggesting the Madame's girls were available for favors in the wee hours of the night, sometimes accompanying men into the woods or down by the riverbank. Meanwhile, Goldie created her own commotion among the travelers by setting up a card table every evening after supper.

Attracting customers was easy; many men yearned for a distraction from trail life. Jason and his entourage were frequent visitors, along with several husbands and would-be miners. Money was exchanged, won and lost, but most of the players were there to catch a glimpse of the fair dealer. To many, the young woman was an elusive goddess—an object of fantasy and desire. Most players found it difficult to focus on the cards, their eyes distracted by her perfect hourglass figure, or the golden curls flickering like stardust by the firelight. Before they knew it, delicate hands would sweep across the table, retrieving their hard-earned coins in a blink of an eye. Nimble fingers would shuffle the deck once again as they fell helplessly under her spell.

Most of the wives were aware of their husbands' late-night activities, and their resentment grew with each passing day. The women made it a habit of gossiping about the outsiders while they washed their clothes by the river, scrubbing away at their washboards in frustration. The watering hole became a gathering place to vent their anger out of earshot of their men. Marjorie Johnson was the most vocal in criticizing Lola and Goldie's shenanigans, stirring the flames of unrest among many of the ladies.

She did not limit herself with voicing her concerns with the women at camp. The grieving mother also shared her indignation with their newest clergy leader, Reverend Jedidiah Mathers. The holy man recently joined the caravan along a feeder trail connecting with Grand Island. Marjorie, having trouble sleeping one evening, wandered about aimlessly until she stumbled upon his calico tent. She waited outside for several minutes, summoning her courage. Taking a deep breath, she pushed opened the flap, and her eyes fell upon her new savior.

❦

ON THIS COLD NIGHT, MARJORIE SAT IN THE FRONT ROW, A TIGHT SMILE hovering over her narrow face, wringing her hands, rocking and moaning as the spirit filled her. Dedicated parishioners threw themselves to the ground, talking in tongues and writhing. Her newfound adoration for Reverend Mathers eased Mrs. Johnson's grief. She hung on his every word, awestruck and wide-eyed, as he prophesized the end of times. His face glistened with sweat as he pounded away at the pulpit, screaming out the horrors of hellfire, drops of spittle spraying over the frenzied crowd. The mousy woman rocked in ecstasy, imagining the two of them transcending the glorious Rapture together.

Chapter Fourteen

Cathy and her friends were unaware of all the gossip swirling about camp. On Sunday evening, Simone and Cat made extra servings of stew and bread, then headed toward the grieving parents' campsite. Mr. Johnson sat by the cooking fire studying the flames. The middle-aged man rarely spoke, his sour expression replaced by a look of apathy. His wife scarcely noticed him. Instead, she fussed over Reverend Mathers, serving him his supper as he studied the Bible. The group surveyed the women as they approached. Marjorie dried her hands on her apron and turned toward the visitors.

"Afternoon, Mrs. Johnson. Thought you might enjoy a break from cooking tonight."

Simone smiled and offered the bowl. Cathy looked back and forth between them, sensing something was wrong.

Marjorie refused to take the meal.

"I've heard some mighty troubling things about the company you've been keeping."

Cathy and Simone exchanged puzzled looks.

"I'm not sure I understand your meaning?"

"Folks have been talking plenty about your camp. Yes, indeed."

"What are they saying?"

"They've been saying many things…that you've been taking up with harlots and gamblers. We've all heard about your special brews you concoct in the cauldron of yours. Seems strange to me…like witchcraft."

The Reverend's eyes narrowed as he stood from his chair. He studied the visitors with a look of contempt, then began to read aloud from his Bible.

"Nahum 3:4—5 Because of the multitude of the whoredoms of the well-favored harlot, the mistress of witchcrafts, that selleth nations through her whoredoms, and families through her witchcrafts."

He glared darkly, his lips trembling with indignation. Cathy and Mrs. Becker gasped, looking at one another with mouths open.

"Surely there's been some misunderstanding."

The man in black stood with his arms reaching toward the heavens.

"And on her forehead a name was written, a mystery, 'BABYLON THE GREAT, THE MOTHER OF HARLOTS AND THE ABOMINATIONS OF THE EARTH.' And I saw the woman drunk with the blood of the saints, and with the blood of the witnesses of Jesus. When I saw her, I wondered greatly. And the angel said to me, 'Why do you wonder? I will tell you the mystery of the woman and of the beast that carries her, which has seven heads and ten horns.'"

The friends exchanged frightened looks, reaching for each other's hands. They turned to leave, but Cat changed her mind at the last minute.

She took a deep breath before speaking, her heart racing as she summoned up her courage. "Father Sebastian taught us to love one another. The Bible says, *Judge not, that we be not judged.* We should love our neighbors as ourselves. Should we not? Goldie, Lola and her girls are our neighbors. They've been nothing but kind and helpful. Why would we shun them?"

Marjorie's pale eyes narrowed as a twisted smile crept over her face. She pointed a finger toward Cathy.

"Your Father Sebastian is nothing but an idolater. Reverend Mathers has made it clear. The priest has soiled his flock with Catholic hypocrisy—worshipping statues of Mary and wooden idols. The truth has been revealed to me. What good has your Father done for his people? Did his prayers and Rosary beads help my poor Bella Jane? No! Lucifer has been well-hidden in his flock of sheep. You've gone and laid down with harlots and idolaters. There's an evil in this camp. Sinful deeds destroyed my precious daughter, and a similar fate awaits those choosing to consort with the devil and his minions. You go back to your bed of harlots and gamblers. Stay away from us, filthy witch!"

Marjorie pulled at her hair in agitation as she regarded the women. Her husband stared off into space as his wife began quoting Bible passages. Cathy and Simone looked on in shock, then hurried to their campsite to escape the madness.

LOLA AND GOLDIE WERE FINISHING SUPPER IN THE FADING LIGHT. THEIR EYES widened when they noticed Simone and Cathy's expressions.

"What's the matter, girls?"

The frightened women took turns describing Marjorie's ravings and the Reverend's fury.

Lola put her hands together, looking toward the river.

"Damn it. So sorry to hear this nonsense is starting again. Not the first time we've gotten heat from religious folks."

Goldie turned away. "Seems like we brought you a bunch of trouble. Maybe we should move the wagons and keep our distance until things blow over."

"Nonsense." Cat looked among her friends for support. "You will do nothing of the sort. We're family now."

Lola's eyes welled up as she took Cathy's hands in hers.

"Ah, you're a darling girl. I'm proud to call you my friend."

Goldie placed her arms around their shoulders.

"This is not the first time we've been scrutinized by the so-called proper ladies of town, nor will it be the last. Just a shame to pull you into our mess."

Mrs. MacGregor moved closer, taking Lola and Goldie's hands in hers, "We've gotten to know you quite well over these past few weeks. You're good people. We won't stand by and let them bully you. You just keep your head high, and we'll do the same."

The friends agreed to stay together despite the growing tensions. They enjoyed a quiet supper while considering the day's events. That evening, Goldie set up her card table as usual, while Jason and his posse took their seats. Her golden waves shimmered in the lamplight, shuffling her cards daintily while entertaining the men with her clever banter. Cathy said her goodnights, making her way to bed. She tossed and turned for almost an hour, unable to sleep. The soothing sound of Goldie's laughter drifted her off to fitful dreams.

Chapter Fifteen

CATHY WOKE UP THE NEXT MORNING WITH A STRANGE PREMONITION THAT something was dreadfully wrong. When she heard Lola's angry swearing, she sprang out of bed and slipped her robe over her nightdress to see what was the matter.

The morning was unusually foggy, with a biting chill in the air. Lola and Goldie were shivering by their wagons with their arms crossed.

"What's happened now?" Cathy asked.

"Look!"

Unbelieving, she stared at the crimson paint. WHORE was printed on Lola's prairie schooner, while Goldie's wagon was covered with the word GAMBLER.

Midnight flew down, landing in a blur of inky feathers. She absently stroked his back as he perched on her shoulder.

"Who would do such a thing?"

"I think we have an idea…but kitten…did you see your own wagon?"

Startled, she turned around and gasped with her hands to her mouth.

WITCH was etched along the side of her vehicle, drops of scarlet dripping from the wooden surface.

Jason overheard the commotion and came outside to see what was happening, his eyes widening when he noticed the crimson letters. He whistled, giving Cathy a meaningful look.

"Seems like you made some enemies, kitty cat."

She bit the inside of her lip, mouth trembling with anger. Before she could speak, Jason stepped closer, taking her hand in his.

"I've got some paint in my wagon. Would you like some help covering over the nasty word?"

She glanced up in surprise. "Thank you. I'd be mighty obliged."

The group turned to see the Cohen family along with Simone and her husband.

They pointed toward the writing as Sheriff Carpenter shook his head in disgust.

"The Reverend's got everyone fired up about hell and damnation. Appears like some of his parishioners decided to take matters into their own hands." He glanced over at the graffiti. "Maybe Father Sebastian can try to reason with him, being they're both men of the cloth."

"I don't think it will do any good." Cathy said. "Reverend Mathers and Marjorie were both ranting about the evils of Catholicism last night. Told us Father Sebastian led his flock astray."

The sheriff's eyes narrowed. "So, you talked to Marjorie Johnson last night then?"

"Yes."

"Hmm…seems a coincidence this occurred right after. It's a real shame what happened to Bella Jane. I know both she and her husband's suffering, but this ain't no good. They can't be attacking others because of their misery. Do you suppose she helped paint your wagons?"

"She was upset the last we spoke," Simone said. Mrs. Becker looked uncomfortable, not sure if she should say more.

Goldie and Lola moved closer, so she wouldn't have to.

"We're to blame," Lola said. "She thinks we're all a bunch of lowlife sinners."

The sheriff looked kindly at the Madame, tipping his hat.

"We haven't any problems from you or your girls, ma'am. I would have been out here before all of this. Figure this is none of my business, but you might want to keep a low profile for a while until things blow over."

"Sounds like a good idea. We'll be having plenty of work once we hit San Francisco. So, we'll keep out of trouble until then," said Madame Vilonia.

"I'm eager to see San Francisco myself once our journey's over. Should be quite interesting," said the sheriff.

"I think I'll put my cards away until things quiet down. No need to get the people all worked up for nothing," Goldie said.

"Good idea. Still have some tough roads ahead of us. The desert will be coming up before we know it, and there's plenty of river to cross. People need to focus on the trail instead of turning on one another." He looked at Cathy with knitted brows, "Young lady, may I have a quick word with you before you get to work on the schooners?"

"Of course, Sheriff."

He led her over toward the water's edge.

"Other than the wagon incident, have there been other problems along the trail?"

"I'm not sure of your meaning?"

"Is Jason giving you any trouble?"

She looked thoughtful before answering, "Been tending to his horse for a while and cookin' for him in the evenings in exchange for his mare. But he's been alright, I guess."

He nodded, then looked out toward camp.

"You just let me know if there's any issues."

She hesitated a moment considering his possible involvement with Bella Jane, glancing at Jason as he carried a bucket of paint over to her wagon. There wasn't any proof he was up to no good, so she refrained from mentioning her suspicions.

"Thank you, Sheriff Carpenter, I'll make sure to let you know if anything strange happens."

"You're welcome, Miss Cathy. I'll be riding out with Shane tomorrow morning for a scouting mission. We're hoping to find some fresher water sources, seeing how sooty the river's been of late. Might be able to locate some streams a little further down. If you have any issues while we're away, be sure to alert the men at camp."

"Appreciate all your help."

The sheriff tipped his hat and headed over to Marjorie's tent for questioning, suspecting she was involved in the painting affair.

As Cathy watched him leave, she wondered why he seemed so suspicious of Jason. *Did he know something she didn't, or perhaps, Shane informed the sheriff about his own concerns?* Either way, the talk left her uneasy.

When she returned, Jason handed her a paintbrush.

"Everything all right?"

"Yes, looks like the sheriff's questioning some of the travelers to see who might be involved in this painting mess."

He gazed down with his mouth pursed, sensing she was holding something back.

Cathy looked away, trying her best to keep her voice steady. Jason made her uncomfortable even in the most ordinary of circumstances.

"Well, thank you again for your assistance."

"Of course, darlin'. I love helping a damsel in distress." He regarded her face, his eyes gleaming. Nodding politely, she looked away, unsettled by the strange energy between them. Jason turned to open the can of green paint. He chuckled to himself.

"Same color as your eyes."

The corners of her mouth rose as she glanced at his wagon. "Looks like we're going to

match."

"Yes, darlin'. We're a pair now."

He held her gaze a moment before getting to work. She dipped her brush and set out to cover the scarlet words. Jason worked alongside Cathy for the better part of the morning, trying to engage her with gold hunting schemes, spinning his tales of adventure he planned on having once he reached Sutter's Mill.

When his stories became more sordid, and offensive, such as rambling on about shooting Indians and massacres, she became unsettled and tuned him out. She imagined his tall tales fascinated his friends, but for her, they were disquieting.

He sensed she was unimpressed and was at a loss on how to get her attention. Frustrated by her lack of interest, he tried a more physical approach —grazing her hips with his hand as he leaned toward the paint bucket, brushing alongside her body as he worked. She was unaware of his intentions, her head still spinning from the idea someone did something so outrageous to her property.

What might happen next? The idea was frightening, and she yearned to see Shane again. Just having him nearby was a sense of relief. By the time they'd covered the last red letter, Jason worked himself into a silent fury. The

Cohens and Beckers having assisted painting both Lola and Goldie's wagons, headed over to check on Cathy's.

"Looks like we're just about finished up thanks to Mr. Edward's help today." He didn't return her smile, but instead, headed back to his wagon without a second look. As they watched him leave, Cathy wondered what triggered his sudden change in mood.

Rachel Cohen looked over with concern, "Is everything alright?"

"Yes, I'm not quite sure about Jason, though. Seems a bit out of sorts."

"Sorry to hear. My husband and I wanted to let you know my family and I will be preparing a Shabbat dinner tonight."

"Shabbat?"

"Are you familiar?"

"Why no."

"In practicing Judaism, we celebrate the Sabbath beginning Friday at sundown and ending Saturday evening with the appearance of three stars. We refrain from work, much like Christians do on Sundays. This is in honor of the Lord's creating the heavens and earth in six days, and then resting on the seventh. It's part of the Ten Commandments—to hold the Sabbath day holy. Mr. Cohen and my family enjoys preparing a special dinner, lighting candles, reciting prayers on Fridays at sundown. We call this Shabbat."

"Sounds beautiful. I'd be more than honored to participate," Cat said.

Lola and her girls gathered around, "Could we join you, too?"

"Of course, ladies. You're all welcome."

THE BULLHORN SOUNDED AS THE CAMP READIED THEMSELVES FOR ANOTHER day of traveling. With the late start, the caravan crossed ten miles by the afternoon.

The Cohens made camp with Cathy and her friends, tying their hefty wagon next to Goldie's. Lola and her girls gathered around to see what they could do to help prepare Shabbat dinner. Rachel asked if they'd mind chopping up the herbs and vegetables for the evening meal. The women went to work slicing up parsley, rosemary and thyme. Knowing Cathy was vegetarian, Mrs. Cohen decided to make potato latkes. Simone offered some fresh eggs from her hens, which she took happily. Cat brought out her onions and potatoes to add to the dish.

Rachel prepared a special challah bread by mixing water, yeast, eggs, flour and salt. Once the dough rose, she divided the mounds into three sections, braided them together and baked the loaves inside a Dutch oven.

Her husband added coals underneath and atop to heat, while the women finished cutting up the herbs and potatoes. Simone brought out her churn, the day's travel having already turned the milk to sweet butter. Donnie was tending to their heifer and calf, leading them down to the river to graze under the orange sky.

Once the dinner was ready, Cathy noticed Jason was absent, so she walked toward his wagon, knocking lightly so as not to startle him.

"Yes?"

"Supper's ready if you'd like to join us. The Cohens have prepared a special Shabbat meal."

"Not interested. Stomach's a little out of sorts tonight."

"Oh, sorry. Could I make you some mint tea? Might help settle it some."

"No, thank you. I'm turning in early tonight. See you in the morning."

"Goodnight then. Let me know if you change your mind on the tea. I appreciate your help today."

"That a fact?"

Cathy's eyebrows rose in question.

"Why yes, I'm mighty obliged."

There was a long pause before he responded.

"Goodnight."

Cathy shook her head, puzzled by the strange exchange, wondering if she'd offended him somehow. Perplexed, she headed back to join the group for supper.

Mr. Cohen offered Mr. MacGregor and Mr. Becker Yarmulke to wear. They took the skull caps, placing them on their heads as instructed. The men helped move cleated boards, nailed together, over ox yolks, which worked as their makeshift dinner table and chairs. Once everyone was seated, Rachel Cohen stood over the banquet and smiled. She proceeded to light two candles and then covered her eyes with her hands, quietly praying. Gently, she waved her hands over the open flame, directing the light toward her face. She prayed. Afterward, she uncovered her eyes and looked out at her guests.

Mrs. Cohen explained, "Dear friends, it's time to greet each other and give welcome."

They turned to one another and embraced. Mr. Cohen answered

"Shabbat Shalom!" as he shook hands with his neighbors. A dark Yarmulke rested atop his golden curls in the fading light. Smiling, he faced the group and began singing in a deep baritone, starting in Hebrew, followed by an English translation.

COME OUT MY BELOVED, THE BRIDE TO MEET; THE INNER LIGHT OF Shabbat, let us greet. Come out my Beloved, the Bride to meet; The inner light of Shabbat, let us greet. "Observe" and "Remember" in a single word, He caused us to hear, the One and Only Lord. G-d is One and His Name is One, For renown, for glory and in song. Come out my Beloved, the Bride to meet; The inner light of Shabbat, let us greet. To welcome the Shabbat, let us progress, For that is the source, from which to bless. From the beginning, chosen before time. Last in deed, but in thought-prime. Come out my Beloved, the Bride to meet; The inner light of Shabbat, let us greet...

MRS. COHEN TURNED TO HER FRIENDS, "LEKHAH DODI MEANS COME MY beloved. It's an appeal for a mystical 'beloved' that could mean either God or one's friends to join in welcoming Shabbat."

On the last verse, the guests were motioned to stand and look in the direction of the woods, greeting *Queen Shabbat* as she arrived. They were instructed to take their seats, and everyone received a cup of wine. The Cohen's eldest son, Joshua, lifted a golden decanter toward the star-filled sky. He sang in a sweet and clear voice.

Praise to You, Adonai our God, Sovereign of the universe, Creator of the fruit of the vine. Praise to You, Adonai our God, Sovereign of the universe who finding favor with us, sanctified us with mitzvot. In love and favor, You made the holy Shabbat our heritage as a reminder of the work of Creation. As first among our sacred days, it recalls the Exodus from Egypt. You chose us and set us apart from the peoples. In love and favor You have given us Your holy Shabbat as an inheritance.

FOLLOWING THE BLESSING, THEY PASSED A BASIN OF WATER ALONG, AND THEY took turns washing their hands. The group watched Mrs. Cohen uncover two loaves of challahs as her husband blessed the bread. A piece was placed on each plate. Once everyone was served, they began talking amongst themselves.

Lola smiled at Mr. Cohen. "Beautiful singing and this supper is something else. I could get used to Shabbat dinner every Friday night!"

"We'd be happy to have you."

Rachel smiled, placing extra potato latkes on the twins' plates.

"Thank you, Mrs. Cohen." They chimed in unison.

Goldie took a sip of wine, sitting back in her chair. "This is mighty fine vittles. Thank you for having us."

"Our pleasure. We're happy to be traveling with you all."

When dinner ended, Mr. Cohen went over to their wagon and retrieved his violin.

He played a soulful melody as the group relaxed under the inky sky. They agreed to set up camp together and would do so for the remainder of their travels.

෴

JASON HEARD THEIR MUSIC AND LAUGHTER FROM INSIDE HIS WAGON. EVERY word, every sound, adding fuel to his building resentment.

Who did she think she was this Cathy Brennan? He'd bided his time. He'd given her work to pay for the miserable pony. Why, to think he'd spent his entire morning painting her wagon while she didn't even give him a second look, spurned him every chance she got. It was bad enough the girl refused to go to supper with him. Every time she denied him, his anger grew. He'd been more than patient, and it was time for the filly to give something back. He'd invested enough time and effort on her. Usually, the deed was so easy, all it took was a smile or glance, and the girl was underneath him, legs spread and begging for more. Not this one though. What did she think anyway? She was too good for him? Daddy always said women had three purposes in life—cooking, cleaning and bedding. He'd tasted her cooking and cleaning; now it was time for the bedding.

If she didn't do it willingly, he'd make her give it up. All he needed was to get her alone in the woods, and he'd have his way with the stubborn girl. Yeah. He chuckled thinking about the look of surprise when he tore her clothes from her trembling body. Maybe she'd put up a real fight when it happened. He felt his manhood aroused by the idea. He'd pay her back for spurning his advances. His mind wandered to the times he'd spied her bathing in the river. Those sleek curves and firm breasts were a sight to be seen. Yes, sir. He was tempted to take her right there but knew the plan was too risky, too many witnesses. But her body was going to be his, and he intended to get his fill. Who did she think she was anyway? The girl saw no problem hanging out with gamblers and whores...even Jews for Christ sake! Why the hell didn't she even glance his way? All she cared about was what Shane thought. Well, he'd teach her things the boy couldn't even imagine. Yeah. Break her in nice and good then turn her loose when he'd finished up with her. The wrangler wouldn't even want her after he was done. Then she'd come crawling back, but he'd send her packing.

He sat on the edge of his mattress, grinning in the fading light, stroking himself roughly, imagining the life dimming from her emerald eyes. The hopelessness on her pretty face would be so worth the wait. Yes, it was going to happen...very soon. He groaned in ecstasy as he climaxed to the image of his fingers around her throat.

Chapter Sixteen

※

CATHY AND HER FRIENDS KEPT TO THEMSELVES OVER THE WEEKEND, reflecting on the strange shift in camp. They decided to keep a close eye on their wagons to make sure the vandalism did not happen again. On Monday morning, they rode together in the arid heat, passing miles of prickly pear and colorful wildflowers scattered along the seemingly endless valley plains. An occasional rattlesnake appeared within the dry grasses, spooking the animals and the men riding them. Every so often, gunfire would go off, as another reptile was left to rot under the blazing sky.

As the wagon train struggled further along the North Platte River, they experienced their first glimpse of Chimney Rock. An impressive column of clay and sandstone rising from the dusty earth like a mysterious pyramid from days gone by. Reaching five hundred feet, the pillar of limestone, clay and ash was a startling milestone. The circumference was nearly half a mile in diameter, creating excitement amongst the travelers.

Two more days passed before they were able to gaze at the natural wonder up close. The caravan camped half a mile away, the afternoon light casting a kaleidoscope of colorful hues along the pyramid-like structure. A host of colorful wildflowers glistened around its base, sparkling like jewels beneath the horizon. A flowing stream was discovered nearby, so they filled their barrels to capacity. Cathy and her friends were overjoyed by the tranquility of their surroundings, mercifully unaware things were about to change in ways they couldn't even begin to imagine.

Chapter Seventeen

Sheriff Carpenter joined Shane on a scouting mission Monday morning. For two days they traveled over the arid prairies along the river's edge, searching for fresh creeks and springs. The pair became frustrated once they'd discovered the river's runoffs appeared just as silty as the main body.

As they headed further west, they noticed discarded furniture and supplies dumped by previous wagon trains. Buzzards circled above, dark sentinels in the dreary sky. As they neared the clearing, a mound of freshly dug earth caught their eyes. They dismounted and approached the site with hats in hands. The grave was four feet in diameter with a small porcelain doll resting at the top. A wooden placard, read,

Cindy Ann Williams, Beloved Daughter of Sam and Patricia Williams, Born August 3rd, 1843–Died June 22nd, 1848

The sheriff shook his head as he read the dedication.
"Poor child."
Shane nodded somberly as they walked along the river's edge, noting the articles of clothing and debris floating in the river. Then the smell hit them. Stuck between a pile of boulders was a decomposing ox. Several buzzards picked at the rotting flesh, while heaps of maggots wiggled and fed,

occasionally spilling into the pungent water below. Sheriff Carpenter looked toward the ground, fighting back the urge to vomit.

"The water's bad. The wind's pushing this filth downstream."

Shane's eyes widened as he imagined the people back at camp. They wouldn't realize the danger until it was too late.

"The river has most likely been compromised for days, seeing the stage of decomposition. We need to get word to the travelers. The water's going to need to be boiled before drinking if we can't find any fresh streams."

They turned their horses around, racing back to warn their loved ones as the buzzards circled lazily in the hazy sky.

Chapter Eighteen

GOLDIE, LOLA AND THE GIRLS JOINED UP WITH THE COHENS AND THE MacGregors every evening for supper. Since the day their wagons were damaged, a division split the travelers into two groups. Cathy noticed quite a few families avoided them, often looking the other way as they passed. Marjorie spread rumors about the women to anyone who would listen, even suggesting Cat was involved in witchcraft. Her eyes would narrow as she described the strange potions concocted in Cat's cauldron and the way the raven followed the girl around like an evil familiar.

The friends grew even closer with the growing vendetta against them. They'd share their plans and goals every evening, promising to keep in touch once they'd made their separate ways. Jason was subdued since the day the Cohens joined camp, often sulking off by himself and avoiding conversation. Yet, every so often, he'd show some interest toward Lola's girls. The young women were wary around him, sensing something was just a little off. Darla seemed particularly troubled by his attention. Something about the man unsettled her, and she confided her fears to Lola one evening after supper.

The Madame listened quietly as Darla shyly voiced her concerns. Afterward, she sought Jason out by his wagon to have a talk, explaining how her girls were no longer available for favors on the sheriff's request. He shrugged it off, but she noticed a flicker of anger in his eyes when she gave him the news.

This was a half-truth since the ladies would occasionally sneak off with some of their favorite clientele when the mood would strike. Darla, however, was reluctant to take on any new jobs, choosing instead to spend her time with a newcomer by the name of Isaac Collins.

Lola met the young man one evening by the river and invited him to join her friends for supper. The group took an immediate liking to him, charmed by his sense of humor and easy-going nature, so they invited him to join their camp. He relished the home cooking and conversation, but his attention was drawn to the petite girl by the fire. Isaac stole glances at Darla throughout the evening, eventually summoning the courage to sit next to her.

They spent the next several hours chatting beneath the starry sky, staying awake long after everyone was in bed. Once Darla felt comfortable, she began to tell her story, unburdening a lifetime of pain and regrets. He listened quietly, allowing the girl to find her voice. When she was finished, he escorted the young lady back to her tent. Before saying goodnight, he reached for her hand, kissing it.

She looked at him in wonder, surprised he didn't ask for more. That evening, Isaac drifted off to sleep with a smile as he pictured her pretty face.

It didn't take long to fall in love with the waif of a girl. He'd seek her company every evening, holding her close under the inky sky. They'd gaze up at the stars, talking of their hopes and dreams, and planning. The young man was aware of Darla's profession but wasn't concerned with the past. A carpenter by trade, he dreamed of building lodgings for the new arrivals in San Francisco. Charming and boyishly handsome, he'd been lucky in acquiring the means to start his business. Darla was amazed that someone so good looking and proper could be interested in someone in her line of work. If she was honest with herself, she was beginning to fall in love with the young gentleman.

Lola noticed the girl's infatuation and wanted her to choose her own life's path. Unlike some madams, she didn't consider her *soiled doves* property but rather charges. She waited patiently for Darla to confide in her about the new love interest. Until then, she feigned ignorance anticipating the day Darla was ready to test her wings.

⊗⊛⊗

DARLA'S PREDICAMENT WEIGHED HEAVILY ON LOLA'S MIND AS SHE JOINED her friends at the riverbank. As they approached the shallow water, the sound of buzzing insects and the smell of rotting debris overwhelmed their senses. They shook their heads when they noticed the trash strewn along the river. Two middle-aged women were filling their buckets as Cathy and Lola headed over. They whispered something behind their hands, then walked past with noses in the air.

"Why, there's some mighty rude people at this camp," Lola said. She shook her head as she watched them leave. "Have to judge others I guess… makes um' feel good."

Cathy grimaced as she noted her surroundings. The water was covered by a thin layer of insects wiggling along its opaque surface. Mosquitoes were everywhere, hovering in transient clouds, waiting for fresh blood. A rosy bump rose on Cat's upper arm, and she scratched it absently. This was not the first time they'd come across the issue; the shallow river was becoming increasingly soiled as they traveled. Hoping the scouts would find some fresh springs, the women filled their pails reluctantly, wrinkling their nose at the unpleasant smell. Ravens landed across the sandbar, pecking lazily at the remains of a rotting trout. Flies covered the carcass, crawling over its flesh in moving shadows. Cathy shuddered, glancing down at her bucket instead.

"Better add some cornstarch to sweeten the taste. We'll let what we collected set a bit."

"Yep, it's a real shame to see people trashing up the river. Why, they're going to go and spoil the water if they keep it up."

Back at camp, the group moved slower than usual. The women were all a little light-headed preparing supper. An uneasy feeling washed over Cathy as she took her seat, meal in hand. She absently picked at the stew, her stomach becoming queasier with every bite. At clean up, Cat noticed how unusually pale the MacGregors appeared.

"Are you feeling alright?"

"Well, actually, my stomach's a bit queasy, dear."

Cathy put her hand against Mrs. MacGregor's forehead and winced at the heat coming off.

"You're coming down with a fever."

"I took some aspirin, but it's not helping much."

Cat looked thoughtful for a moment. "Maybe some mint tea will settle your stomach some. I'll add feverfew leaves to cool you off. Let me make you both a cup before I finish cleaning camp. She used water from the rain barrel for the tea, suspecting the river water was spoiled. Cat studied the MacGregors with concern. They seemed to be fighting to keep their eyes open as they finished their cups.

Cathy took their mugs. "Perhaps you should turn in early tonight. You both seem quite peaked." She noticed the beads of sweat rising on their foreheads.

"Thank you. Our supper tasted strange tonight." Mrs. MacGregor looked at Cathy with a soft smile. "You've been awful good to us, dear. I want you to know. Hope we didn't use up all your fresh water."

"No, it's not a problem. I still have half a barrel along with a bit from the spring last week. Planning to save some for the desert. Sheriff said we're due to pass some barren land just outside the Rockies. I'm starting to think I should have used fresh water in our stew tonight, seeing the river water's so silty." Cat said.

"Maybe. It's hard to know when you're trying to ration. Can't imagine how awful it would be to run out completely." She looked over at Cathy, offering a gentle smile. "You've been a blessing to us both."

She studied Mrs. MacGregor with concern. There were still hundreds of miles left to travel. *Why did it feel like she was saying goodbye?*

"Are you sure you're alright? I'd be happy to make another pot of tea."

She reached out her gnarled hand and took Cathy's. The skin was hot and damp.

"I'll be sayin' my Rosary tonight. The good Lord will take care of us as he always does."

"Please, if you need anything, just knock on my wagon, even if it's late."

"Sounds smart, dear. Try to get some sleep. You look a wee bit peaked yourself." Mrs. MacGregor gave Cat a quick peck on the cheek and patted her hand. "You're a good girl. Been mighty fine traveling with you and Shane. He'll take good care of you."

Cathy watched her climb into the wagon while her husband reached for her elbow with trembling hands.

"Let me know if I can make you anything else...I've plenty more herbs."

They said they would, then disappeared behind the partition. Cathy finished cleaning and said goodnight to her neighbors. Her stomach was rumbling by the time she'd lowered the canvas cover. She reached for a tin cup and dipped it inside the rain barrel, then sprinkled a piece of mint leaf on top.

Just as Cathy was falling asleep, her eyes darted open. She was barely able to make it out of the schooner before doubling over in pain. Cat stumbled blindly in the dark, feeling her way over the dry earth, then squatting down in relief. Diarrhea was followed by waves of nausea. She vomited violently onto the sandy gravel, as her head spun. With her heart pounding in her ears, she winced. When the spell passed, she wandered in the dark. She glanced at the MacGregor's wagon, worried they might be ill, but there was nothing but silence. Afraid to disturb them, she crawled inside her schooner instead. After chewing on a bitter feverfew leaf, she lowered herself down to bed, praying her stomach would settle. She tossed and turned for over an hour before falling into a fitful sleep.

A young girl searched the forest floor. In the fading light, she caught herself along the thorns, crying out in pain as they pierced her delicate skin. A drop of blood dripped from the tip of her finger, lost in a sea of brambles. Ravens perched high in the birch trees cawing loudly, as she stood frozen in place. A hand reached out to caress her shoulder as she considered her mother's face.

"Don't worry about the weeds in the garden; focus on the flowers, child. Look for the purple bells."

Sunlight pierced through the forest canopy, illuminating emerald leaves. She grinned, reaching toward the fuzzy stems, her fingers grazing over the treasured bells.

Chapter Nineteen

CATHY SAT BOLT UPRIGHT IN BED, A TREMBLING HAND PUSHING AWAY A LOCK of ebony hair from her sweaty face. Her stomach churned as the room spun out of control. Fumbling absently with the wagon cover, she found her way outside, blinking in the bright sunlight. She stumbled a few yards before her legs buckled, as she retched up a thin stream of bile. Trembling beneath the blazing sun, the world swam in chaotic circles. *How could it be so late in the day? Where was everyone?* The answer was just out of reach. *The water... there was something in the water. Don't worry about the weeds in the garden; look for the flowers. Search for the purple bells.*

Beads of sweat rolled over her face as she wiped her mouth with her hand. Another wave of nausea dropped her to her knees. She sat for several minutes until the stomach cramps passed. *Why hadn't the bull horn sounded?* The terrible retching sounds across camp soon answered her question. *The water is tainted.* By the time she'd gotten her vomiting under control, word was spreading about the illness.

Cathy went back to her wagon to fetch a glass of fresh water. With shaking hands, she added a dash of sugar and salt, along with lemon juice, honey and mint leaves. She let the tincture set for a bit before drinking it down. When her head was clearer, she gathered her ingredients and carried them over toward the cooking fire. Mrs. Becker was helping Donnie climb out of the wagon; both mother and son looked pale and flustered.

She turned to Simone. "Have you seen the MacGregors this morning?"

"No. I've been up all night with Donnie. He's terribly sick, and I'm not much better. Haven't seen either of them."

Cathy looked toward their wagon.

"I better go check on them."

As she walked closer, she noticed a strange buzzing sound. She knocked lightly on the bottom board. When there was no answer, she climbed up into their rig and called their names. Still nothing. With a trembling hand, she pushed open the canvas barrier and peered inside. The room was dark and heavy with sickness.

She squinted in the dim light, climbing inside the wagon with her hands splayed. Flies swarmed her field of vision as she moved toward the backend of the carriage. Her stomach lurched as the room spun. *Oh no, God. Please don't let it be*. Ears pounded to the pulse of her racing heart. The MacGregors were curled up together under the blankets; a gnarled hand hung loosely over the mattress. A strand of Rosary beads was resting on the floor. Cathy pulled back the covers and began to scream.

ᘓᔓᘔ

POWERFUL ARMS LIFTED CATHY FROM THE FLOOR AND THEN OUTSIDE, AWAY from the sorrowful sight. Holding her to his chest, Shane embraced her as she sobbed inconsolably. Sheriff Carpenter and Father Sebastian climbed inside the MacGregor's wagon to pay them respects. The elderly priest made the sign of the cross over their bodies, praying for the departed souls.

Cat looked up at Shane with tears welling in her eyes, "Mrs. MacGregor said she wasn't feeling well last night. I offered to make her some tea but didn't realize how serious it was."

"You couldn't have known, Cat. The river's gone rancid several miles up. Found a dead ox decomposing in the bank. We'll need to make a detour around the river for fresher springs. There's a shallow crossing not far from here. Might be our best bet."

Cathy's vision blurred as he continued speaking. She could hardly understand what he was saying as another voice echoed from the past.

Look for the purple bells.

Foggy memories surfaced, just out of reach. She strolled along a dimly lit forest with a dark-haired woman by her side.

Don't worry about the weeds in the garden. Look for the purple bells. Find the pretty flowers, child. We need the roots to bring back to the village. The plants will help with the stomach sickness. She lowered herself to the ground, trying her best to avoid the prickly brambles.

A purple bell-shaped flower was clustered deep in the ground, surrounded by green stems moist and sticky.

"Momma, I found one!"

"Good girl! It's the wild ginger root we've been searching for."

Cathy realized what she needed to do, and there was no time to spare. She started to speak, then gasped as she noticed her fiancé's pale face.

"Let's get you back to my wagon. Better lay down."

Once inside, she led him to the mattress as he doubled over in pain. Cat wiped his face with a damp cloth and offered a glass of fresh lemon water. She pulled the quilts over him once he'd drained the glass. "Stay put until I get back. I have an idea that might help with the stomach illness."

He slipped deeper under the covers as chills set in. Cathy glanced back, reluctant to leave, but decided this was their one hope. She kissed him on his cheek, noticing the heat coming off, then grabbed a basket with scissors and headed outside. Mrs. Becker was kneeling next to Donnie as he struggled to stand.

"Just gave him some laudanum, there's quite a bit left if you'd like to share."

"Thank you. Shane's awful sick, too. I have a barrel of fresh water we can use for infusions to bring down the fevers. We'll want to gather some more ingredients. I'll explain more when I get back."

"Where are you going?"

"Into the woods. Say a prayer I find what I'm looking for. It could be the answer we need."

Simone watched as Cathy entered the dark forest, brushing across piles of leaves in the hope of finding a cure. She searched for over an hour until the fluttering of wings made her glance up. Midnight landed next to her, scratching frantically until he uncovered a glimpse of purple.

"You found one!"

The wild ginger bells rested just above the soil, surrounded by soft, hairy heart-shaped leaves enfolding a bell-shaped flower. Taking scissors in hand, she clipped the reddish-brown ginger from their hairy stalks. Once her basket was full, she turned to stand as a shadow fell over her. Jason stood behind, grinning.

"What are you up to, kitty cat?"

He offered his hand, helping her to her feet.

"I think I might have a cure for the stomach sickness. Found some wild ginger. It can be made into tea and should help with the stomach pains."

He stared without blinking; then his eyes dropped toward her breasts.

Cathy felt a cold shiver run down her spine.

"I better go back."

She attempted to leave as he reached for her elbow. "Don't rush off just yet." He turned around, pushing back a lock of hair from her face.

"You have such beautiful eyes. I bet you know it, don't you? The pretty one always does. Just look at your ebony hair…mighty fine. I bet you like to take your time brushing those ringlets at night, considering your mirror. Do you admire yourself in the glass? I imagine so."

A tightening sensation clawed at her throat. She took a deep breath, trying not to panic.

"Have to head on back to the wagon now. Shane's awful sick. I need to go…"

"I bet the boy loves to stroke your silky hair. Do you let him run his hands through your curls?" He moved closer, weaving his fingers through the strands. "Maybe he likes to touch you in other places, too?" He chuckled as his bright eyes widened. "Do you enjoy it, Cat? Do you like to be touched by men?"

Her lips trembled; *I need to go back.* Cathy stared up at his cold eyes heart pounding as he held her firmly by the arm.

"I think you've been teasing me, kitty cat. I've been patient, biding my time, waiting for you to warm up to me, but my patience's run out now You're going to give me something, girly girl."

A cold tremor run down her spine as he stared.

"Is it true what they say? Are you a witch? Maybe you put a spell on m because I can't stop thinking about you."

"I don't have time for this! Need to get back to camp. Shane's ill."

As she turned to walk away, he grabbed her painfully by the shoulder.

"Your boy can wait. I think it's about time you experienced a real man."

"Leave me alone!"

He cupped a hand over her mouth as she struggled, stifling her screams.

"You can cry all you want, but I don't think anyone will come. Half the camp's puking their guts out, some might even be dead, and quite a few of the lady folks think you made deals with the devil. It's kind of funny how Marjorie talks about you and your friends. You're not very popular around here, Cat. But it's okay. I like you just fine. I'll treat you real nice if you're good. Maybe I'll even make you purr, little kitty."

Her eyes bulged as she fought to loosen his hand from her mouth, gasping for breath.

"Yes, sir. The way I see it, you already have a bad reputation for hanging out with whores and gamblers. Why don't you at least enjoy some guilty pleasures if you're being blamed for um' anyhow? What you say, kitty cat… are you ready for some fun?" He cupped his hands around her buttocks as she raked his face with sharp fingernails.

"You little bitch!"

She took his surprise as an opportunity to pull away from his grasp and went running down the hillside, slipping along the wet leaves. As she neared the riverbank, she noticed a great oak rising toward the heavens. Dozens of ravens perched along its milky branches, watching her with their onyx eyes. Her lungs burned as she raced toward the ravine, the murky river just a few yards away.

He caught up with her just as she reached the bank, grabbing her by her long curls. She cried out in pain as he shoved her against the base of the tree.

"Get off me!" She clawed at his face as he laughed.

"Oh, God…I do love a fighter!" He pushed her arms above her head, holding them in place by their wrists. "Yes, real nice." His tongue caressed the hollow of her neck, then flickered down toward her heaving chest, ripping open the bodice as his teeth grazed over the delicate skin. "You taste so sweet. We're going to have a real nice time."

Cathy tried to pull away while staring up at eyes, which appeared like empty husks in the fading light. Everything was so familiar.

"You'll see, darlin'."

He groaned as he traced his fingers under her dress.

"Be a good girl and just…let it happen. We can take our time if you want. I'll be sweet if you are. But, girly girl…if you struggle too much… well…we can do this the other way too." He traced his lips against her ear. "I'll tell a secret." His eyes widened as he pressed down with his hips. "It will be more fun if you fight." He cupped her breast with his right hand and kissed her mouth roughly. Jason paused a moment, propping himself up on his elbows.

"I almost forgot something." He reached his hand into his pants pocket, retrieving a pink ribbon which he dangled in front of her wide eyes.

"You be a good girl, and you can have this pretty bow." He placed the velvet tie across her glossy hair while planting a kiss on her quivering lips.

"Bella Jane sure loved her ribbons. Yup. Silly girl didn't put up much of a fight like you do. She was mighty willing to please me. Just like taking candy from a baby…gave it up nice and quick. Course, the whiskey helped the first time. Yes, sir. We had our fun…until the day she told me she was expecting. Little bitch threatened to get me kicked out of camp. Can you imagine? Wanted to tell her daddy."

He looked down and grinned, biting down on his bottom lip.

"I didn't mean to kill the girl." He chuckled, recalling the memory. "Just wanted to shut her up, so I covered her face like this." His hands pressed down over Cathy's mouth and nose as she struggled, tears streaming down her face.

"Are you going to be nice?" She shook her head, gasping for air, clawing at his fingers.

"Real good. No need to start crying now."

He moved his hands away from her mouth as she coughed and choked. Once she'd caught her breath, she looked up trembling, pupils dilating.

"You…killed her?"

"I did," he said. "Strung her up and made it look like a suicide. Wasn't too difficult to get her up in the tree. The storm kept everyone inside, and the girl didn't weigh much. Worked out nice and easy."

"You're a monster."

"Do you think so, darlin'? Well, I guess you're about to find out." He pinned her down with his knee as he fumbled with his trousers with one hand and pushing up her dress with the other.

Her vision blurred as the old memories surfaced. *She was a child again, running alongside her mother. She found it difficult to see in the smoky haze; her eyes burned as they tried to find their way to the river. Her father bent down to kiss her freckled nose. Then he was saying goodbye as a bullet tore through his neck. There was so much blood…and her mother called his name. Momma was being pulled away kicking and screaming. The pale man with bright eyes dragged her to the great oak tree. She was crying. The stranger was hurting her; she wanted to help but didn't know how. Mother whispered, run. Blood-curdling screams echoing in the wind as she rushed blindly toward the cold, dark woods.*

The images were replaced by beating wings. Cathy looked up as Midnight flew down from the tree, landing on the top of Jason's head, and went to work pecking his face. There was a blur of blood and feathers as the man screamed in terror, trying to protect his eyes from the painful beak. Deep gashes opened across his skin as the bird pecked. The sharp crack of snapping twigs made Cathy glance over her shoulder as three Indian men appeared from the bank. She gasped as they stared in her direction. Midnight stopped his attack and flew to her shoulder.

Jason panted, wiping his face as he glared at Cathy, trails of blood streaking down his cheeks.

"What the hell? Maybe you are a witch…Jesus Christ. You're going to pay, girly." He hissed, lunging forward and grabbing her foot. She shrieked as Jason looked past her shoulder in disbelief, his eyes focused on the strangers. His mouth fell open as they watched him silently.

"Well, would you look?" He smiled, his tongue darting at the corner of his mouth. "A bunch of Indians have come a calling. I'm finally getting my chance to kill some dirty redskins. Yep, today's the day."

He absently licked the blood from his bottom lip as he reached for his gun. Yet, he was too slow, for the arrow was already making its way toward him, piercing through his Adam's apple in one fatal blow. His eyes bulged as he reached for his throat, clots of blood bubbling down his chin as he lurched over. Cathy stood trembling in shock as a hand settled on her shoulder. She gazed into familiar eyes.

"You're safe now, Little Raven. Everything will be all right." He leaned down, kissing the top of her head. Afterward, she watched in amazement as the three warriors disappeared back into the forest.

Ebony wings filled the sky, descending upon the corpse in a blanket of glossy feathers. Cat gasped as dozens of ravens began picking apart Jason's face, tearing it up into meaty strips. One bird successfully dislodged his right eye from its socket and proceeded to gobble it down in juicy gulps. He cawed triumphantly once he'd finished, then worked on the remaining one.

Cathy turned away in horror and ran with her basket of ginger grasped in her right hand. She could still see the image of his bloody face as she fled.

Chapter Twenty

Sheriff Carpenter was chatting with Simone and her husband when he noticed Cat emerging from the woods. His eyes widened at the sight of her torn dress and wild eyes.

"Miss Brennan, are you alright?"

Tears streamed down her face as she ran toward them.

Mrs. Becker put her kettle down and wrapped her arms protectively around her friend. Shaking uncontrollably, Cathy pointed toward the forest with a trembling hand. "Jason attacked me, but I was able to get free."

Simone gasped as the sheriff's face darkened in anger. "Good Lord… looks like the son took after his father. He always was a no-account scoundrel."

Cat glanced up, questioning. Once she'd caught her breath, the sheriff continued.

"I knew Jason's pa. He was found murdered outside a saloon just on the border of the Nebraska territory. Happened a couple of years back. He'd come around town every so often, boasting about killing Indians and looking for deputy work. Used to tell a story how he'd aided the government in burning down an Indian village back in the 30's. I didn't want to judge the son by the father…but I should have kept a closer eye on him. Jason's pa, Percy Edwards, started hitting the bottle with a vengeance when he couldn't find work. There were rumors he took out his frustration on his family with his fists. Eventually abandoned his wife and son altogether, had no choice but to ride out on a rail.

"I figured it wasn't my place to judge, but I couldn't shake the feeling there was something a little off about the boy. I know Marjorie's hands were full keeping her daughter away from him, too. It's a real shame."

"Sheriff, I have something awful to tell you…about Bella Jane."

"Oh?" He raised an eyebrow.

"Jason confessed he'd killed her after she threatened to tell her father he'd gotten her with child, said she'd get him thrown out of camp if he didn't make it right for her. He choked Bella Jane to death. Made it look like a suicide."

Simone Becker made the sign of the cross and shuddered. "Oh…dear Lord. Poor girl."

Sheriff Carpenter focused on the line of wagons, biting the inside of his lip. "Her parents need to be told. Do you suppose Jason's hiding out in the woods? I can send a search party if he's taken off on foot."

"No…he's dead."

The sheriff and Simone exchanged shocked expressions.

"He was shot with an arrow…it all happened so fast. Jason pinned me down beneath an oak tree when a group of Indian men appeared out of nowhere."

"Indians?" The sheriff appeared thoughtful but not surprised. Cathy looked at him in confusion, sensing he was holding something back.

"Yes, they saved my life. I know it's strange, but the man who shot Jason looked very familiar to me."

"How so?" He folded his hands under his chin as he awaited her answer.

"Well, it all happened so fast. Their hair was tied back in long braids. also noticed some strange symbol on their arms and chests." She looked between her friends, trying to find the right words.

"They saved me. I can't even imagine what would have happened without their help." She shuddered as Simone caressed her shoulders, looking down with sympathetic eyes.

"Thank God, you're safe. You'll be just fine."

Cathy looked up, comforted by her friend's reassurance.

"Well, I don't have any idea how they stumbled upon us, but I'm so grateful they rescued me from something so terrible." Tears filled her eyes. "The tallest of three shot an arrow through Jason's neck as he was reaching for his gun. He died right there under the oak. It was so horrible…and then the strangest thing happened."

Simone rubbed her back. "What happened, sweetie?"

"The man with the bow looked at me and spoke."

"What did he say?"

"He said, 'You're safe now, Little Raven. It's going to be all right.'" Cathy turned to see Father Sebastian standing by her side.

"There's something I need to discuss with you, young lady. Something which should have been told years ago."

She gazed at the men in confusion, then glanced over at her wagon. A muffled groaning came from inside.

"Oh, my God, Shane needs me!"

Mrs. Becker put her hand on her arm. "I checked on him a few minutes ago, and he's running a fever. Gave him some aspirin and laudanum. Been calling out to you while you were in the woods. Donnie's getting worse, too. Can't keep anything down." She said, eyes glistening with tears.

Cathy's forehead wrinkled with worry. "I better go check on him." She turned to leave, then turned back toward her friends.

"I forgot to show you something." She held up the basket of ginger. "I found these in the woods, plan to make a tea to help with the sickness. We'll need to gather as much fresh water as possible from the wagons. I have half a barrel from the spring. Simone, I'll go in and mix you up an infusion with lemon, sugar, salt, honey and mint. The drink should bring down Donnie's fever and keep him hydrated.

She nodded in relief as Cat rushed back to her wagon.

"Miss Cathy, would you mind sharing your recipes with the camp later? People are mighty sick."

"Of course, Sheriff."

"Good. The caravan's not traveling today. Too many ill right now, so we better stay put until we get a handle on things."

Lola approached with her girls behind her. They looked pale but eager to offer their assistance.

"We want to help, too. Just tell us what to do."

Cathy looked thoughtful for a moment, trying to think. Her head was still spinning from the attack in the woods.

"My plan is to make batches of tea and water tinctures to bring down the fevers and rehydrate those suffering. Girls, grab baskets and search for these.

You can find them buried in the forest. Look for the purple bells." She held up a clump of ginger. "Bring back as many as you can. We also need more lemon, honey, mint, sugar and salt. I have some in my wagon, but we'll have to gather more if this sickness is spreading through camp. Perhaps the men can help collect fresh water from the travelers and boil any taken from the river. Probably need some extra pots as well. Gather up as many lemons as you can. I purchased a basket of them at the store in Fort Kearny, but we need more. Bring these supplies back, and we'll start making batches of teas and infusions."

"Cathy, there's one last thing before you go," the sheriff said. Cat shifted her feet, eager to get back to Shane. "Mr. MacGregor and his wife entrusted a letter to me. They asked me to give it to you if something happened to them."

She looked down and closed her eyes. With everything going on, there wasn't any time to properly grieve.

"When Shane is feeling better, you should read it."

"Thank you, Sheriff." Her eyes glistened as she studied the sealed envelope.

"I'll be back later to check on you."

Cathy climbed into her wagon, dropping the letter inside a wicker basket. She discovered Shane curled up under the quilts, flushed with fever.

"I'm here, darling."

Her hand shook as she pushed back the damp waves from his forehead, kissing his cheek.

He looked up and reached for her hand, eyes widening when he saw her tears and torn dress.

His forehead wrinkled in concern. "What happened?"

"Nothing to worry about, love. I'll explain later after you're feeling better." His eyes slowly closed as his fever spiked.

She went to the rain barrel and removed the lid. Her hands trembled as she reached inside with a tin cup, squeezing half a cup of lemon juice, along with a pinch of salt, sugar and a spoonful of honey. Shane managed to sit up and drank the infusion. "I'm going to make you a tea to help you sleep."

He nodded absently, looking across the room in confusion.

She sorted through the hanging baskets to retrieve a few lemons and mint leaves. They'd be added to the ginger tea along with a little honey and sugar.

Mr. Becker kept the fire going as the women made batches of ginger tea and lemon infusions. Cathy brought a kettle-full back for her fiancé. Shane took a few sips before laying down. The women worked day and night helping their sick loved ones. Lola's girls took turns bringing the remedy to their neighbors. Most of the travelers were so desperate they took it without question. Goldie visited each wagon instructing the families how to create their own tinctures, while Lola and her girls delivered batches of ginger tea. When they passed Marjorie Johnson's wagon, they heard dreadful moans coming from inside. Darla held the kettle, while Lola knocked on the sideboard.

Marjorie looked out from the awning with a scowl. She climbed down, brows knit and hands on her hips. The women glared at one another without speaking. Darla broke the uncomfortable silence. "We've brought you some tea for your husband. We've got some more back at camp…" Before she could finish her sentence, Marjorie rushed over, knocking the copper pot from the girl's hands. The ladies watched in shock as the precious liquid soaked into the dry earth.

"Harlot, take your devil potions and be gone!"

Darla's eyes glistened with tears as she bent down to collect the kettle. Lola reached for the girl's hand, and they headed to their wagons in silence.

Chapter Twenty-One

CATHY STAYED WITH SHANE THROUGHOUT THE NIGHT, COOLING HIM DOWN with water-soaked towels and spooning him drops of the remedy. He tossed and turned in his delirium, his fever spiking at midnight. She silently prayed over him, desperate for any signs of improvement. On the second morning, sunlight flooded the open spaces of the wagon as he struggled to sit up.

"Shane, you're awake!" She put her cool hand to his forehead and sighed in relief. "The fever's broken! Thank God."

He reached his arms out toward her as she snuggled against him. They held each other for nearly an hour as they listened to the cawing of ravens outside the wagon. Shane stroked her hair, kissing her tenderly.

"I better get started on breakfast. You're going to need to get your strength back. Oh, and before I forget, the sheriff left a letter for us...from the MacGregors."

Shane nodded soberly.

Cathy climbed down with her kettle, then gasped as she noticed piles of food and supplies surrounding her wagon.

"What on earth?"

Simone and Lola were sitting by the fire with coffee in hand. They looked up as Cathy headed over.

"What's all of this?"

"Something ain't it?"

Lola grinned, shaking her head. "We received some gifts as well." She pointed toward their carriages. Several baskets of breads, flour and cans of beans and vegetables, were stacked near the front-right wheel. "Seems like we've gotten back into the good graces of our fellow travelers. Their loved ones are feeling better, so I figure they want to thank us. Can't look a gift horse in the mouth...my momma used to say."

"Truly amazing. I'm happy to hear everyone's recovering."

"Well, most are doing fairly well. Not everyone..."

"Oh?" Cathy looked up startled.

"Yes," Simone said. "The sheriff stopped by a few minutes ago. Seems like we'll be having another funeral today."

"Oh, dear God. Who's passed now?"

"Marjorie's husband."

"Oh, no." Cathy wrung her hands, looking toward the wagons. "Why couldn't she just have accepted our help and put her pride aside for the sake of her family?"

Lola wrung her hands, shaking her head. "Yes, and there's more."

Cathy's eyes widened.

"She's gone."

"Gone?"

"Yup. Took some of her belongings and pulled foot with Reverend Mathers. Don't figure she'll be coming back anytime soon. The woman's plumb lost her mind. Several wagons left last night, followers of the crazy holy man. Must have turned back from the trail, most likely heading eastward."

Cathy was speechless. She wouldn't miss Marjorie Johnson, but she felt sorry her husband was left behind without a proper burial. The task would fall to the sheriff and his crew.

The women prepared breakfast, tired but relieved.

Simone brought over a bag of flour and a cup of oil. "Donnie's feeling much better. Scared me something awful to see him so sick. We're all mighty grateful."

Lola's girls were making their way out of their tents. They looked exhausted but satisfied.

"Good morning." They said between yawns.

Simone studied Cathy with admiration. "Where did you learn to make these teas and infusions? I didn't have a chance to ask the other night."

"This is such a strange story. I don't know if you'll even believe me."

"Of course we will." Lola and the girls shook their heads in agreement.

She took a breath, glancing at her friends. "I dreamed how to do it."

Simone's eyes widened. "You are a special young lady." The women gathered around Cathy as she summed up the courage to continue.

"The night before we all became so ill, I had the strangest dream. There was a mother and child in the woods. They were looking for ginger root. A lot of this is hard to explain…so much I can't even begin to understand. There were these…visions or memories. I could see a forest, and everything was so very familiar."

Simone put her hand on her friend's shoulder. "The Good Lord works in mysterious ways, mademoiselle."

She smiled, relieved by her friends' support.

"I've been having some bizarre dreams over the past few weeks." She watched her friend mixing flour, baking powder, a serving of butter and milk, along with a pinch of sugar and salt, and three fresh eggs from her young hens, Henny, Penny and Sky. The pullets were enjoying some sunshine inside their wooden crate beside the cooking fire. Cathy studied the birds as they scratched the ground, pecking at pieces of ground corn spread over the grass.

"My ladies have been laying nicely the last couple of days, maybe since we've taken a break from traveling," Simone said. She cracked an egg into the batter, then poured the mixture into the skillet. The liquid bubbled and sizzled as it touched the hot surface.

Cat beamed as she noticed Shane walking over to the group.

"Mornin' ladies."

The women waved, relieved to see he was feeling better.

"Nice to see you're back on your feet, son. Looks like your woman took good care of you." Lola said.

Goldie climbed down from her wagon looking refreshed, her golden curls glowing in the soft morning sun, a rosy blush on her high cheekbones.

"Feeling any better?"

"Yes, thank you. The tea helped my stomach last night. Mighty obliged. Sorry, I slept in so late. Let me help get breakfast started."

She hurried her way toward the cooking fire and began peeling a basket of potatoes. Her hands moved over the spuds, freeing the skins in graceful sweeping arcs. Cathy looked on in awe as she worked her way through the basket in mere minutes. She realized Goldie was as skilled with a paring knife as with the cards she dealt. Lola's girls took turns cutting up the potatoes and adding them to the iron skillet. Simone's husband and son were just making their appearance when breakfast was being served. They hurried over when they smelled the flapjacks and fried potatoes. Cathy was relieved to see Donnie's color was back as well as his appetite. Rachel and her family were the last to join them. Mr. Cohen insisted his wife take a seat while he served her. She was up all night with her sons, worrying over the sick children. The boys looked better, but their mother appeared exhausted. Cat offered Rachel a cup of tea. She took it gratefully, smiling and nodding in relief.

The friends took turns filling their plates and sat down by the dying fire. An icy wind blew back their hair as they sipped hot coffee. The women watched as Shane and Donnie gobbled down their meals. Simone spooned out more flapjacks for her son and husband, offering them warmed maple syrup from a pitcher. They immediately started in on their second helpings.

Cathy looked thoughtful a moment before speaking.

"Your son's looking much better. I was thinking he might like to have Jason's mules...since...he won't be needing them anymore. Donnie's so good with animals, and I know he'd take care of them."

Simone looked over at her son. "I think he'd like that very much. It's a wonderful idea. Lord knows those poor animals would appreciate a tender hand."

She went over and explained what transpired while he was ill. His eyes widened when he learned about Jason's death and the attack in the woods. When his mother was finished, he jumped from his seat and rushed toward the cooking fire.

The boy's eyes glistened with tears. "Miss Cathy...are you, all right?"

"Yes, Donnie. I will be. Do you think you might like the mules for your own."

"I'd be honored."

"Good. Perhaps we'll tie um' behind your parents' wagon, for now, unless you think you might want the carriage.

His face grew serious as he looked over at the abandoned schooner.

"No, Miss Cathy. I don't want nothing of his. The mules are a different matter...seeing they're innocent creatures and all."

"They'll be mighty lucky to have you care for them." Cat said.

When breakfast was over, the group cleaned up and sorted through their new supplies donated by the thankful travelers. Shane moved the bags of flour and beans underneath the covered wagon as Cathy eyed the cans of vegetables. She shook her head, amazed how quickly things could change in such a short time. When her fiancé finished loading the wagon, Cat went to her desk and retrieved the letter.

She looked up. "Should we open it?"

"Yes…I suppose we should. Can't imagine what this is all about. Just seems unbelievable they're gone."

Cathy considered the white envelope while tears blurred her vision. Her hands shook as she unsealed the letter and read aloud.

May 24, 1849, The Year of Our Lord

   Dear Cathy and Shane,

   If you're reading this letter, then it appears the Good Lord has taken Mrs. MacGregor and I into his loving arms. Please don't be suffering with the news. We began the journey in the hopes of meeting up with our daughter in Monterey. The doctor warned us the trip would be quite difficult. Our one wish was to embrace the time left with one another.

   Cathy, I've appreciated all you did for the Misses with your teas and herbs. Your kindness was such a comfort to her these past few months. As you well know by now, Mrs. MacGregor has been suffering terribly with the rheumatism, and I have not been very well myself. Our doctor diagnosed me with a bad heart some time back. Time was running out for the two of us, so we wished to visit our family one last time. We hoped to spend the remainder of our time left with them. But, if you're reading this letter, the dream was not meant to be.

   We've grown so fond of the two of you during this journey. You reminded us so much of ourselves at your age, so very much in love and not two pennies to rub together. Our daughter and husband have done quite well for themselves in Monterey. They manage a large rancho by the sea. Last year, they built a second cottage overlooking the ocean. This is where we were going to live out our final days.

   So, please go over to our wagon after you've read this. Inside you'll find an envelope, the key to the cottage and the property deed.

   We bequeath you our home to start your lives together. There's a second letter in our wagon we'd appreciate you giving to our family. Their address is written on the envelope, so if you could mail it along at the next outpost, we'd be grateful. We wish you all the happiness marriage and love can bring.

Along with the cottage, will be passin' along the wagon, mules and life's savings. Our daughter and her husband are well off, and it wouldn't make much of a difference in their lives. So, we'd like to give the money to the two of you as an early wedding gift. It's not a fortune by any means but should help you get started. We know Shane must work the cattle drive, but we've asked Donnie to drive the wagon for you if something was to happen to us. He promised he would. The boy's a fine lad, and we know he'll do a good job.

Mrs. MacGregor and I wish you a blessed marriage and beautiful life. We're mighty happy to have traveled with such a caring young couple.

God Bless,

Mr. and Mrs. MacGregor

"Oh, Shane."

Tears streamed down her face as he pulled her close.

"I can't believe it, Cat. Such a kind and thoughtful gesture."

A knocking on the wagon made them both jump. Cathy pushed the cover open and saw it was Father Sebastian. He looked up, his hand covering his eyes from the glaring sun.

"May I come inside and chat with you for a moment?"

"Of course, Father."

"Thank you, dear. I came here today to discuss some well…rather personal things."

He glanced over at Shane.

"It's alright, Father. Anything you have to say is fine. We're getting married soon."

"Oh, joyful news!" Father Sebastian studied her a moment before speaking. "Well, I've come by to talk on a delicate matter. Perhaps you'd might like to sit down." Cathy's smile faded as she took a seat at the edge of her bed, glancing toward her fiancé.

"Do you remember much of your early childhood, Catherine?"

She looked at her hands before answering. "I've started to remember bits and pieces."

"There was a massacre on an Indian village in the '30s. The tragedy happened not far from this camp."

Cathy winced as her stomach tightened.

"Shall I continue, dear?"

"Yes, please go on."

Father Sebastian looked down in concern.

"A fellow priest and I were camping nearby. The village was destroyed, most of the people died. Simply terrible. We could hear their distant cries in the night." His eyes glistened with tears.

"Well, I imagine you're wondering what this story has to do with you." He searched her face, trying to find the right words. "There was a little girl lost in the woods…she saw the light from our camp and made her way to us."

Cathy bit her bottom lip as the memories surfaced.

"Should I go on?"

"Yes, please."

The child was very brave but traumatized from losing both her parents. Later, we met up with the sheriff in town to find out if any of her people survived. There were a few Comanche's left from the massacre, but most perished. A warrior named Running Dear, described the attack and mentioned he was looking for word of his niece, Little Raven."

Cathy's eyes lit up as she recognized the name.

"Father, the man in the forest called me, Little Raven."

The priest nodded. "We discovered your mother and father were killed during the massacre."

He considered her eyes as they widened in understanding.

"Cathy, the parents who raised you were your adopted parents."

She closed her eyes, trying not to panic. Shane put an arm around her shoulder, kissing her on the cheek.

"Your mother was a healer. She befriended the villagers and later married the chief's son.

My father was Indian?

"Yes…a Comanche warrior. A handful of villagers escaped. Running Deer was knocked unconscious. When he awoke, his tribe was decimated. A local doctor was tending to his injuries when we found him. Dr. Steven Carpenter treated him with great risk to himself, seeing how the townspeople were not accepting of the Indian residents. He said he'd been searching for his green-eyed niece, a child named Little Raven. Once he felt safe speaking with us, we learned the warrior was your father's older brother, your uncle, in fact. Said he'd been having dreams of your mother, Catherine. In his visions, she asked him to watch over you."

Cathy looked up in bewilderment, her mind spinning with questions. *How was it all possible?* She wondered, glancing between Shane and the elderly priest.

Father Sebastian continued his story after giving Cat a moment to collect herself.

"He spoke very highly of your mother whose maiden name was Elizabeth Green. She was known to be a great healer among her people along with her father, a town doctor who offered medical assistance to the Indian community. Father and daughter were well-respected in the tribe, and in return, the natives shared their knowledge of healing herbs and natural remedies. Your grandfather took your mother along with him on his visits to the village. She was eager to learn everything she could about medicine, and during this time she befriended a boy named Raven Eye. Their friendship grew, eventually becoming romantically involved. They attempted to keep their relationship a secret, but word leaked out. There were rumors it may have been the catalyst of the attack on your village. The townspeople could not stomach the idea of a white woman living among Indians.

"Your parents were unaware of the danger and soon married. Elizabeth continued her work in medicine, becoming a respected healer in the tribe. Your father's sister, Flying Eagle, was very close to both you and your mother. Running Deer explained you often joined them in preparing natural remedies. They taught you healing skills from the time you could walk. Your uncle always referred to you as *Little Raven,* although he did mention your mother often called you *Cathy.*

"After we talked to Running Deer, we decided to take you to the nunnery in Wyoming. We couldn't find any remaining family in town. Your grandfather, Dr. Robert Green, passed away the previous year and there was no village to return to following the attack. Your people were decimated in the fire and massacre; the few remaining survivors became nomadic. Your uncle was very torn by the decision but agreed this was your best chance at good life. His one condition was he might see you from time to time. thought our plan would work if he watched from a distance, so we planned to meet up once a year at my church. He was always careful, so as not to interfere in your new life. These moments gave him peace, knowing you were being so well cared for. In fact, the two of us became quite good friend over the years, and I've enjoyed his annual visits. He stopped by earlier this year around Christmas."

Cathy glanced over at Shane.

"I mentioned we would be taking the trail in the springtime. He must have been tracking us, might be why he was able to assist you in the forest."

"Father, it was a miracle. Running Deer saved me from Jason. He was…"

The priest's eyes glistened as he reached for her hands.

"There, there, child. You most definitely have angels watching over you."

Cathy smiled, squeezing his hand.

"Thank you, Father."

"Well, Cathy…there's not much more of this story I can tell you. The nuns took very good care of you and found an older couple looking to adopt. Your new parents tried for many years to have children, but the good Lord made other plans. Because of your Indian heritage, they decided it would be best to move far away. People can be cruel, Cathy, and they feared you'd be judged by your Indian ancestry. You've seen the consequence of prejudice and intolerance in this very camp. We are all God's children, yet there are those who still don't accept this reality. Have peace in knowing both your biological and adopted parents loved you dearly, young lady."

Cathy was overwhelmed by the story. Suddenly her dreams all made sense. She wished desperately to see her parents. There were so many questions still needing answers.

"Catherine, I'm always here for you when you're ready to talk. I'm sure this is all quite confusing and may take a while before it makes sense. Please, pray for guidance. God's always ready to listen."

Shane led Father Sebastian outside, then turned toward his fiancé who was trembling at the edge of the mattress. He took her in his arms as the tears flowed forth. Once she'd gathered herself, he listened patiently as she unburdened a whirlwind of thoughts and feelings. Everything came flooding out at once—the pain of losing her adoptive parents, the guilt over failing to save her mother and the MacGregors, all her worries and fears since they began their journey. When she went on to describe the attack in the woods, he went rigid as she explained Jason's attempted rape and the murder of Bella Jane.

"He's lucky he's dead." He hissed between clenched teeth, "I'm so sorry I wasn't there for you. The bastard!"

"He can't hurt anyone ever again," she said.

Cat tried to erase the image of his bloody face from her mind, a nightmare which would haunt her for the rest of her life. She wept openly as Shane whispered words of love and encouragement, brushing her hair back, kissing away the tears.

"It's all right."

"I've lost my mother and father all over again. The memories keep flooding back, and it's all so confusing." He held her close as she wept in his arms.

"We're going to create our own beautiful memories, darlin'. We have a few more weeks of traveling and then..." Before he could finish, they heard a soft knock on the schooner.

Sheriff Carpenter was outside with hat in hand.

"We're set all set for the MacGregor's and Carpenter funerals...and Jason's." They joined the sheriff, and together they walked toward the west bank of the river.

Father Sebastian gave a touching eulogy under the cool shade of the birch trees. Cathy's body shook as fresh dirt was shoveled across the wooden coffins. They were the last to leave, silently praying over the graves of their dear friends. Cat looked over at Jason's mound and shuddered. With a heavy heart, they wandered back toward camp together.

Chapter Twenty-Two

Shane rode alongside Cathy's wagon for the next couple of days until he was strong enough to join the other wranglers. After two days of riding, the terrain became desolate, fewer trees and a hot wind, which reddened their skin and dried their eyes. On the third day, a startling discovery was made casting shadows of doubt over the exhausted travelers. They spotted several freshly dug graves by the bank; many picked over by wildlife. Flies hovered above a partially decomposed ribcage. The caravan stopped briefly to bury the sun-bleached remains. Father Sebastian prayed over the graves before the schooners were on their way once again.

The following afternoon they stumbled across Scottsbluff, a massive outcropping of rock larger in size than anything discovered in their journey thus far. Looking at the formidable mound gave them courage they were getting closer to the final stretches of the expedition. They took a moment in quiet reflection before traveling onwards.

Afterward, the moving village followed the Robidoux Pass, avoiding the badlands. The caravan followed the narrow trail intersecting with the Wildcat Hills Range, meandering over a lush valley where they gathered wood and fresh water. The valley connected to a summit, which offered their first glimpse of the Rocky Mountains.

Cathy and her friends watched the sunset over the majestic range in silence. A peaceful calm settled over them as they viewed the orange and pink rays cascading over the hillside. The group slept soundly under the star-filled heavens.

Refreshed by the picturesque setting, they rose early the next day eager to finish their trek. The teams followed a narrow mountain pass where they discovered a trading post and loaded up on supplies. Later in the day, they camped near a fresh spring, a welcome relief from the silty water of the Platte. They filled their barrels before leaving the next morning.

After three more days of traveling, they arrived at Fort Laramie alongside the Laramie Mountain Range where North Platte and Laramie rivers intersected. The military base offered adobe-covered mercantile stores, a blacksmith shop and mail depot. The prices were high, but the travelers paid what they could. Shane and Cathy visited the postal building and mailed their letter to the MacGregors' daughter.

Several traders were offering goods to the travelers outside and around the fort. The couple noticed an elderly Indian woman selling colorful textiles near the blacksmith shop. Cathy studied her native garb, contemplating what her life might have been if her people survived. *Where would I be now?* The vendor looked up with dark eyes full of curiosity, gesturing them to come over. The couple sorted through the various blankets and quilts, admiring the unique designs.

"This is beautiful," Cat said. She held up a woven rug, covered in green and white patterned textile with diamond shapes and geometric patterns.

Shane glanced down with a smile. "Would you like this for our new home?"

"Oh, it would be perfect. Yes, please."

Shane paid for the rug, adding a little extra change as a tip. The seller beamed in gratitude as she took the coins, flashing a toothless smile.

Cathy continued searching through the collection, looking for a gift for Rachel. "My friend is expecting. Do you have any small blankets…for an infant?" She demonstrated the size with her hands.

"For baby?"

"Yes."

The elderly woman smiled, reaching for a tiny quilt near the bottom of the stack, holding it up for the lady's approval.

Cathy studied the bright yellow and white blanket, admiring the cheery hues.

"Yes, I love it! Thank you."

She reached in her basket, retrieving her purse. After paying, they glanced up as Mrs. Becker was coming out of the mercantile shop. Donnie was walking beside her, holding a package wrapped in brown paper. Both mother and son appeared nervous, nodding hastily, then hurrying off without a word. The couple glanced at one another, shrugging at the odd exchange and continued shopping. They took their purchases back to camp, noticing their friends gathered around the Becker's tent. Lola's girls giggled as they approached, glancing at one another in excitement.

Goldie waved them over.

"Come on out you two love birds, we have a few ideas we'd like to be sharing."

Cathy glanced at Shane, wondering what was going on.

"We've all been through some hard times for sure these past months." The friends shook their heads in agreement. "So, we've been chatting and came up with an idea we'd like to share with you all."

Goldie folded her hands under her chin, trying to find the right words. Her soft blue eyes glistened.

"As you know, we'll be going our separate ways once we reach San Francisco."

They looked at one another in silence, dreading the thought of saying goodbye. "So, before the time comes, we want to get you hitched up right and proper!"

Lola's girls giggled with their hands over their mouths. Before the couple could answer, Donnie rushed over with his notebook in hand.

"Miss Cathy, it would be an honor if you'd let me help make your wedding dress." He pointed toward the sketches with a shy smile.

Simone walked over and put a hand on her son's shoulder. "He's been working on these since the day his fever broke. What do you think?"

Cathy studied the etchings, impressed by his skill and technique.

"Why these are divine!"

He blushed, relieved she approved.

"I think it's a wonderful idea," Shane said.

Cathy's eyes sparkled with excitement. "I'll have to get some material for my dress. I don't have anything suitable to wear."

Simone took her hand. "We have a surprise for you." She moved toward the wagon as her husband retrieved a brown-paper package tied up with string.

"What's this?"

"Why don't you open it?"

Cathy smiled, wondering what was inside. She removed the wrapping, then gasped.

The women sighed as they studied the delicate material.

"What on earth?" Cat's fingers grazed over the expensive fabric.

"Donnie and I stopped by the mercantile today. We purchased a few yards of satin and lace for your wedding dress. We can go back and pick another pattern if you have something else in mind."

Cathy's tears welled up as she considered her friend's face.

"The material is gorgeous. I can't even begin to thank you."

Rachel Cohen took her hand. "I have a veil if you liked to wear it. The antique was passed down to me from my grandmother from Germany."

The bride-to-be's eyes glistened with tears, overwhelmed by their kindness.

"Oh, it would be an absolute honor. Thank you."

Goldie, Lola and her girls gathered around excitedly. Darla's face froze when she realized Shane was glancing at the fabric.

"I believe it's bad luck to see the bride's dress before the wedding." Her large brown eyes widened with worry.

"Of course," Shane said. He turned away while Simone put the material back in the box.

Darla looked relieved when the fabric was out of sight of the groom. "The girl's always been so superstitious," Lola said. "So, what you say...are we gonna have a wedding?"

The couple looked at one another and grinned. "We think it's a marvelous idea!" Cathy glanced at the other women. "I'd love for you all to be part of the ceremony. Girls, your dresses should be finished in a couple of weeks so...perhaps you'd like to wear them in the wedding?"

They squealed in delight, glancing over at Lola to make sure she approved of the idea.

"Let's break out the gowns for the nuptials!"

"Wonderful! Simone and Rachel, I would love to have you both as m matrons of honor. The women nodded in excitement. "Lola and Goldie would you be my maids of honor?"

The friends gathered around Cathy, placing their arms around her shoulders.

"Of course, doll," Goldie said. Her mouth quivered as she regarded her friend.

"You're going to make a beautiful bride," Lola said.

The friends talked excitedly about their plans for the wedding, staying up past their normal bedtime. They were thrilled to have something happy to celebrate. Little did they know things were getting ready to change for the worse.

Chapter Twenty-Three

Cathy tried her best to focus on her wedding plans as the trail became more vexing. Shane was back to working the cattle drive, so she was often alone with her thoughts and worries. The arid landscape west of Fort Laramie was intolerable to both man and beast.

Exhausted by the evening, they pushed themselves to complete the more important chores such as cooking and washing. It took all of Cat's willpower to work on the gowns after supper, often dozing off with needle in hand. Donnie assisted whenever he could, though he was busy with the added duty of caring for the MacGregor's wagon and mules. Yet, the teenager was determined to finish the wedding gown, even if it meant drinking extra cups of coffee at night to make it happen.

With water scarce and grasslands lacking, the caravan no longer enjoyed the luxury to rest on Sundays, so they pressed onwards for fresher prairies and streams. Father Sebastian offered Bible study in the evening, but most travelers were too exhausted to attend. As the desert stretched onward, many of the frontiersmen feared they were beginning to go mad. Their minds would play tricks along the meandering valleys, sometimes even imagining seeing water in the distance, only to find out they were cruel mirages.

Thousands of grasshoppers peppered the barren landscape along with an occasional sage grouse or rattlesnake. The lack of grasslands made traveling difficult on the animals. As they passed numerous carcasses along the way, they worried about their own stock surviving. Buzzards picked apart fallen oxen in the merciless heat, a gruesome reminder of the perilousness of their journey. So, it was quite the shock one afternoon when the scenery changed, finding themselves at the base of the lush Sweetwater Valley. Marking the impressive site, was a massive granite dome covering five acres of prairie land, just west of Fort Laramie in the Wyoming territory.

Independence Rock was about one hundred and thirty feet high, nineteen hundred feet long and eight hundred and fifty feet wide. The enormous monolith was an important milestone for the travelers since reaching it by July 4th meant they could bypass the winter storms along the mountain range. The travelers prepared a celebratory supper, as their livestock enjoyed the rich grasses surrounding the massive outcropping. Shane was able to take a night off and joined Cathy and her friends.

The pioneers took turns etching their names onto the rock with pine tar and charcoal the following morning. Afterward, the young couple kissed in the shade of the mound, just inches away from their signatures. Another milestone conquered.

❦

THE NEXT DAY, THE CARAVAN REACHED THE SWEETWATER RIVER. THE flowing waters covered a green valley, covered in lush grasses, but absent of trees. Their mules and oxen roamed over the landscape, devouring the fresh greens. Sharp outcroppings of rock were scattered over the trail and passes, so they were careful not to get caught along the treacherous path. The plains were covered in sage grass, as well as ravines of volcanic rock. An alkali dust covered the travelers and supplies, burning their throats and noses. Donnie was burdened with breathing issues by this time, so Cathy made him tea whenever they stopped.

The moving village crossed the river several times until it arrived at South Pass and the open area between the Wind River Range.

Along the snow-capped peaks of the Wind River Mountains appeared a fast-moving creek filled with chunks of floating snow; leftover remains from the July meltwater. They'd arrived at the picturesque landscape overlooking the Continental Divide.

They summited up the rocky hillside with caution. The caravan weaving over sharp outcroppings and treacherous trails made the task daunting. There was great relief when they reached Fremont Peak overlooking the pristine waters below, a rocky landscape covered in wildflowers. Shane met up with Cathy later in the evening and agreed the area was the perfect location for their wedding. They positioned their wagons close to the rushing stream, enjoying the soothing rhythm of tranquil waters. Shane made sure to camp toward the end of the caravan so he wouldn't see his bride before the wedding.

Cathy went to bed filled with nervous excitement, tossing and turning before falling into a fitful sleep. A heaviness hung in the air despite the cool waters below.

ଊୠ

THE GIRLS ROSE EARLY IN THE MORNING TO PREPARE FOR THE NUPTIALS, eager to help Cat get ready for her big day. Lola offered powder and rouge, while Darla braided strands of wildflowers into her ebony locks. As the ladies encircled the blushing bride, Goldie held up a satin-covered jewelry case.

"Cathy, these pearls were given to me by my ma, thought you might like to wear um' as your something borrowed."

"Thank you kindly. I'll take good care of them."

Her eyes welled as her friend placed the delicate beads around her neck.

Lola handed the bride a small paper box while her girls giggled and fussed.

"Well, kitten, I expect you be needing something blue, so I wanted you to have this here garter. Purchased it awhile back at a fancy French boutique. Figured I might use it someday for my own wedding…but those plans seem far away. So…do you think this would suit you?"

Cathy studied the delicate fabric. "Oh, my, Lola, it's awfully pretty. Yes, I'd love to wear it."

The Madame lowered herself to the ground, hoisted the layers of satin and lace while slipping the garter over Cat's shapely leg.

"I think your husband's going to enjoy this just fine."

Cathy blushed as she imagined he would.

Simone stepped closer, admiring the gown. "Well, I guess the wedding dress is something new."

"Thank you, it's beautiful. Donnie's so incredibly talented. I'll never be able to thank him for all of his hard work and kindness."

Simone nodded, with tears in his eyes. "He's a good boy. My son thinks mighty highly of you. He was thrilled to help with your dress."

Rachel Cohen approached with an embroidered length of fabric. "My grandmother's veil will look lovely with your dark hair."

"Oh, this is divine."

She placed the laced covering over her flowing locks. "Perfect."

Cat studied her friend's swollen belly, realizing she was due anytime now. The girls led Cathy outside into the warm sunlight. Colorful wildflowers surrounded the trail, along with the scent of fresh pine. The wedding party accompanied the blushing bride down a mossy path overlooking the cool waters below. Shadows were setting across the Rocky Mountains as the sky began to darken. Mr. Cohen played Mendelssohn's Wedding March on his violin as Lola's girls lifted her train over the uneven terrain. Their colorful gowns of rose, gold, emerald, scarlet and turquoise, appeared like a cheery bouquet in the afternoon light.

Shane stood at the top of the hill, dressed smartly in a grey suit and tie, gifted to him by Simone's husband. His eyes brimmed with tears as Cathy floated over the daisy-lined path, clutching a bouquet of pink wildflowers, which matched her rosy cheeks, a vision in white.

◈◈◈

FOLLOWING THEIR TENDER VOWS, FATHER SEBASTIAN PRONOUNCED THEM man and wife as their friends clapped and cheered. The couple kissed passionately under the stormy sky while the ground quaked beneath them Sounds of joyful celebration turned to frightened gasps as a herd of mountain goats thundered past. Other animals followed close behind—antelopes rabbits and several white-tailed deer.

Sheriff Carpenter sniffed the air, considering the smoke-filled sky. He turned away from the wedding party, sucking in his breath.

"It's a Northern."

Shane's eyes widened as he considered his bride. The horses and oxen agitated by the fleeing animals began to rear and kick.

Cathy glanced up in confusion, wondering what was happening.

"Cat, there's fire on the horizon. Can you smell the smoke?"

Her eyes widened in understanding.

"The cattle will run off if we don't move them."

Her lips trembled as she studied his face. "You need to go."

"Are you sure?"

"Yes, my love."

He reached for her, sweeping her close beneath the darkening sky." Shane kissed her forehead as he stroked her cheek.

"Stay close to the Beckers and Cohens. The men can help with the mules if they start to panic."

Donnie walked over with his head held high. "I can help watch over Miss Cathy."

"Thank you, Donnie. I mighty appreciate it."

The sheriff blew his bull horn, and the wranglers hollered down the line. By this time, several cowboys were moving toward the herd.

Several heifers and bulls broke free, stampeding and kicking up clots of dirt in their panic. Shane saddled up Kelpie, turning him toward the fleeing cattle. Man and horse disappeared into the smoky haze while Cathy watched them leave, tears blurring her vision. With a heavy heart, she hitched up her team, then joined her friends as they steered their wagons across the mountainside.

❧

THE FIRE WAS MOVING QUICKLY NOW, FLAMES BURNING THROUGH THE wildflowers and sagebrush while the sun appeared as an eerie orange disc in the hazy sky. Cathy tried her best to focus on her driving as her wedding dress floated about her body in the hot wind. Another wagon pulled alongside hers. As she glanced at the Beckers, she noticed Rachel appeared unusually pale, her hand clutching her stomach. Biting her lower lip, she fled across the hillside as thunder rumbled in the distance.

Lightning streaked across the crimson sky, as the heavens opened, hail plummeting down across the caravan. The oxen, panicked by the thick smoke and ice, fled across the quaking mountains.

❧

SHANE LOOKED OUT ACROSS THE RUGGED TERRAIN, HIS BREATH HITCHING AS

145

he realized the impending danger. The edge of the cliffside was fast approaching, a steep descent looming over the jagged rocks below. His pony strained in the smoke-filled air, struggling to catch up with the herd, flanking the leading steer in the process. He managed to turn the frightened animals from the cliff, but his relief did not last long. Just as he'd maneuvered them from the edge, a high-spirited bull clipped his horse's flank, causing him to lose control of his pony.

While his horse bucked and kicked, Shane tried his best to stay in the saddle. His head whipped back and forth as he rocketed skyward, releasing the reins as he pummeled down toward the jagged earth. He hit the ground with a terrible thud, breaking several bones in the process. In wide-eyed shock, he gazed over the side of the mountain as his feet dangled down. Seeing the precarious drop-off, the cowboy pulled himself away from the ledge, clutching handfuls of dense sagebrush for traction, crab-walking away while his injured leg dragged behind him. His boot snagged on a clump of prickly pear as he shuffled, causing his ankle to turn at an unnatural angle. The dry pop of snapping bone was followed by a blanket of grey light. As the world disappeared, the amber sky rumbled above, pummeling torrential rains down from the heavens.

Chapter Twenty-Four

THE STORM WAS TREACHEROUS, HAIL FALLING MERCILESSLY DOWN ON MAN and beast. Snow flurries soon followed, a startling contrast from the weeks spent in the arid desert. With the threatening weather conditions, the caravan pulled up alongside the glassy lake once the fire was contained. Cathy and Donnie tied canvas barriers over a line of cedar trees to protect their animals from the snow. Afterward, the bride squinted at the darkening hillside, searching for word of her husband.

Moments later, a figure came racing out of the smoky haze. Mr. Cohen waved his arms frantically, trying to get her attention.

"Rachel's gone into labor. She's in terrible pain. I…don't know what to do." Tears welled in his eyes. "Could you help her?"

"Of course."

Cathy discovered the mother-to-be writhing on top of her mattress, clutching her belly in agony. She rushed to her side, and took her hand, wincing at the touch of her icy skin.

"I'm here, Rachel. Let's try to warm you up." She reached for a quilt, covering her with the heavy cloth.

"Thank you."

A powerful cramp seized her body as she doubled over in pain. The friends climbed inside the wagon and rushed to her side. Meanwhile,

Rachel's husband gathered up his boys and began collecting firewood, trying to distract them from their mother's cries.

Simone reached for Rachel's hand.

"I was there when my sister gave birth. It will be alright, just breathe."

As Cathy studied her friend, shadows from the past echoed from long ago. Women from her village gathered around a young maiden in the throes of labor. The din of her mother's voice floated past as she assisted in the birth, bringing forth the newest member of their tribe.

The memories slowly faded as she listened to her friend crying out in the night.

Feeling more confident, she knelt by the bedside, taking Rachel by the elbow. "I know this might sound strange, but it will make the labor easier if you sit up.

"I trust you."

The friends helped Rachel move to the edge of the bed, propping up her back with pillows. There was a tap on the sideboard. Simone opened the covering and waved Darla inside.

"Could I help you, ladies?"

They smiled and nodded. The girl rushed to the basin for a wash towel, which she dipped into the cool water.

"You'll be fine, ma'am." She gently wiped Rachel's forehead with the damp cloth. "Your husband's outside pacing and waiting for word."

"Yes, he always gets so worried..." She whimpered, unable to finish her sentence.

Darla's eyes widened in concern, looking to Cathy for guidance. She headed to the washbowl and rinsed her hands before checking on her friend.

"Better see how you're progressing...may I?"

"Yes." She clenched her jaw in pain. Cat lowered herself on her haunches and pushed up the nightdress.

"You're beginning to dilate, but you shouldn't bear down just yet."

"I'll try." She groaned as another contraction wracked her body. Simone held her hand as she struggled.

"Everything will be just fine, Mrs. Cohen," Darla said. She rubbed the small of her back, trying to ease her discomfort.

"Thank you for your kindness." She pulled in a deep breath, trying her best to endure the pain.

The women encircled their friend, offering their love and support. Rache appeared so frail they wondered if she'd have the strength to deliver when the time came to push. Her friends stayed by her side, comforting her with words of encouragement. At midnight, Cathy checked the progress and seeing she was fully dilated, made eye contact with the other women.

"Rachel, it's time."

Straining and panting at the edge of the bed, the exhausted mother pushed as the baby began to crown. The women drew closer, lifting her with their love. They were all sisters, forming a link within an endless chain. She drew from their strength, and within the throes of agony, a blessed child entered the world.

❦

THEY DRIED OFF THE NEWBORN WITH SOFT TOWELS, WRAPPING HIM IN THE blanket that Cathy purchased back at Fort Laramie. The infant's aquamarine eyes matched his father's, along with his golden curls.

"Looks like you have another son, my friend." Cathy smiled, handing the baby to Rachel.

The mother cuddled the tiny bundle as tears swam down her face.

"Oh, he's so beautiful."

Simone pushed a lock of damp hair from his forehead. "Beautiful like his mother."

Darla gazed down in wonder. The women were relieved to see their friend at peace.

"Do you have a name in mind?" Cathy asked.

She studied the pink babe cradled close. "Yes. I'm going to call him Isaac David Cohen. He'll be named after my pa."

"A fine name," Goldie said. "I expect your husband is having a time outside. Should we give him the news?"

"Please."

Simone opened the wagon cover and called down to the family. Mr. Cohen hurried toward the wagon with his two sons in tow. Once inside, he planted a kiss on his wife's cheek as he caressed the curls of his newborn son."

Once they'd tidied up, Cathy and her friends said their goodbyes to the happy family. The boys surrounded their mother, gazing at their baby brother in wonder.

SHORTLY AFTER LEAVING THE COHEN'S WAGON, THE YOUNG BRIDE LIT HER lantern and wandered through camp, searching for her husband. Lulling of cattle suggested the herd was contained, but Shane was nowhere in sight. Once the snow flurries tapered off, the friends gathered around the fire, offering Cathy a fresh cup of coffee.

An hour of nervous conversation transpired until they heard hoofbeats approaching. Cathy jumped to her feet, her eyes widening when she noticed Sheriff Carpenter riding his palomino, her injured husband slumped over the saddle.

"Shane!"

"Your husband's a hero, ma'am. Saved the entire herd from stampeding over the cliff

but was mighty banged up in the process. Busted his leg something awful...some ribs broken by the looks of it."

She bit down hard on her bottom lip at the sight of his battered body. They helped him down from the horse, as Cathy cried out for her friends' assistance. The men gathered around, then lifted him up and carried him inside her wagon as he groaned.

"Please be careful." She winced as they laid him down on the mattress. The pain was excruciating, but he did his best to remain calm as to not upset his wife.

"Don't worry, darlin'. Not as bad as it looks."

She kneeled toward his ankle, her eyes widening when she realized the severity of the injury. With a pair of donning scissors, she cut the pant leg up to his hip, wincing at the sight.

Sheriff Carpenter shook his head. "Going to have to be set. I've done i before...a while back when one of my deputies was injured in a robbery."

Mr. Cohen looked down with eyes full of sympathy. "I've got a piece o spruce we can use to help bind. Let me go fetch it."

"Mighty obliged."

Cathy glanced up at the other men, her hands shaking as they grazed ove his shattered leg. "Do any of you have some whiskey? The stronger, th better... this is going to hurt, I'm afraid."

Mr. Becker wrung his hands before answering. "I've got a jug of the ol orchard back in the wagon."

He glanced at his wife. Her eyes narrowed when he mentioned having alcohol. "I'll go and fetch it."

Once he came back, Cathy poured a generous amount in a tin cup and brought the whiskey over to Shane.

"Drink up, love."

He did as he was told.

Once he'd drained the cup, the sheriff looked at Cathy.

They each took a side of his leg, feeling for the lines of the break. In one quick motion, they moved the bone back in place as he hollered in pain. His skin was a greyish hue, from shock, his pupils dilated.

"I'm so sorry," Cat said. She fought back tears as she looked down at his pale face.

He bit down on his bottom lip with his eyes closed. "May I have another drink?"

"Of course." She poured him a generous round, and he took it eagerly, downing it in one gulp.

Once the whiskey was gone, she cleaned his chest and body with fresh water and soap, then bound his ribs and ankle with leftover material from her wedding gown. When he was wrapped up tight and warm, their friends said their goodbyes, leaving the newlyweds some privacy on their wedding night.

"Not quite what I was picturing for our honeymoon," Shane said.

"We've always done things a little differently. There'll be plenty of time once you're back on your feet. Thank God you've come home to me."

He offered a tranquil smile and took her hand. "I'd never leave you, love. You're my life now."

Tears rolled down her cheeks as she leaned over, kissing his warm lips. He tried to sit up, grimacing in pain. Cathy admonished him. "You lay back down this instant, Mr. Mackenzie."

"Yes, ma'am."

"I know this isn't easy, but you have to stay as still as possible to let your bones mend. Probably going to take a couple of months. If you can do this, you should be able to walk unaided by the time we hit Monterey." He studied her face, with a lopsided grin. "I can do it...as long as you're here by my side."

"Always and forever."

She smiled down, kissing him on the forehead, then pulling up the covers around his chin. Once he was comfortable, Cathy changed out of her soiled wedding gown, slipping on a cotton nightdress over her chilled body.

"You're so beautiful."

Shane's eyes filled with longing as his wife cuddled up next to him on the mattress. She listened to his heartbeat while breathing in his clean scent. He was asleep within minutes, snoring against her warm body. She let out a deep sigh and said a prayer of gratitude for his safe return.

Chapter Twenty-Five

THE NEXT SEVERAL WEEKS WERE FULL OF LONGING AND FRUSTRATION. Cathy, having finished the girls' dresses, discovered more leisure time in the evenings, so she used the extra hours to tend to her husband's every need. Feeling useless, Shane offered to help Cat with driving but was admonished every time he asked. His young wife was determined for him to mend safely, even if it meant he went crazy in the process. The friends took turns helping her husband out of the wagon at rest stops along the trail. He was in quite a bit of pain, sudden movements causing him terrible discomfort. Donnie assisted his father in carving out a pair of crutches from a leftover spruce beam. Shane was grateful for the thoughtful gift and put them to use. They were helpful over short distances, although his ribs were still sore to the touch, along with a sprained wrist, which made maneuvering the crutches difficult. Bathing required Cathy's help, which she was more than happy to do. Sores erupted on his calf where the splint was beginning to rub.

Concerned for infection, she washed the irritated skin every night before supper and applied a rosehip salve to the abrasions. She padded the brace with sheets of satin from leftover fabric to buffer the wooden supports. Shane shook his head, complaining he smelled like perfume and was wrapped in ladies' garments. Cathy kissed him on the cheek as he grumbled, trying her best to cheer him up.

Fearing his leg would become infected, she made sure he soaked it daily.

Luckily, the waters were fresh as they traveled alongside the Rockies. His evening baths took place behind canvas coverings by the water's edge. As he sat in the chilly currents, Cathy would wash his body, her hands grazing over his muscles as she kissed his neck.

He enjoyed the attention immensely, yearning to sweep her off her feet, but unable to. There were times her eyes would linger over his suntanned body, admiring his firm muscles and well-defined physique. He'd see the desire in her sparkling eyes and try to draw her closer, but she'd admonish him, fearing he'd hurt himself in the process. So, they continued their marriage life unconsummated to their mutual frustration.

To hurry up the healing process, Cathy collected herbs along the trail to add to her collection, experimenting with a variety of tinctures and salves. She scraped bark from the birch trees along the trailheads along with rosemary branches, which she mixed into a fragrant mixture.

By the glow of the lantern, she massaged the solution along his legs, ribs and tired muscles. When she'd finished, he held her close against his warm body, kissing her tenderly. Just as they were beginning to doze, a knock on their wagon startled them back to reality. Cathy opened the canvas barrier, surprised to see the Beckers outside with a pot of tea.

"Hope we're not bothering you. We have something we'd like to discuss if you have the time."

Shane sat up in bed as his wife let them inside. After pouring the tea, the friends took their cups and sat down. A few moments later, Mr. Becker walked over to Shane, patting him on the shoulder while handing him an envelope full of money.

Shane looked up, questioningly, wondering what was happening.

"We can't begin to thank you for saving our herd during the firestorm. Don't know what we'd have done if they'd perished. Most of our life's savings tied up with the cattle.

"Not a problem, it's my job."

Mrs. Becker considered the injured wrangler. "You did more than your fair share. We're sorry about you getting hurt. We'll never be able to truly thank you, but we brought along your payment for the work, along with a bit extra. Of course, we don't expect you to do any more wrangling while you're healing, but we have a position ready for you after arriving in Monterey.

"Mighty obliged."

Mr. Becker studied his face. "We want you to be the overseer of the wranglers if it suits you. Pays double."

Shane's eyes widened in surprise.

"Yes, I'd love the position."

"Wonderful news! Just heal up now, and we'll work out the details later." The Beckers stood up and said their goodnights. Cathy and Shane thanked them again before they left the wagon.

With the weight of their work over for the time being, along with the money the MacGregors left them and the payment from Lola, the newlyweds could relax somewhat, knowing they earned a sizable savings. In many ways, their intimacy was growing stronger, since the bond was not just a physical, but an emotional connection tying them together. They held each other contently, planning for their new life by the sea.

Chapter Twenty-Six

WHILE THINGS WERE SETTLING DOWN IN CAMP, A FEW MEMBERS OF THE caravan were having their own personal awakenings. Donnie was more confident after taking over the responsibility of driving the MacGregors' wagon and caring for his mules. Along his travels, he made a friend during the visit at Fort Laramie. Jeremiah Smith was heading to the San Francisco territory, eager to carve out a piece of the city for his own. Handsome and self-assured, the newcomer was determined to make a name for himself. The two were soon inseparable, meeting up each evening for supper, camping their schooners side-by-side at nightfall.

On his eighteenth birthday, Donnie's mother made her son a chocolate cake and invited their friends to join her family in the festivities. Jeremiah Smith was one of the guests in attendance. Quick-witted and charming, the young man was welcomed into their group.

He was passionate as he spoke, explaining his dream of traveling to the San Francisco territory and opening a successful mercantile shop. With all the gold flowing into town, he imagined the miners would be needing supplies for their expeditions. A small inheritance from his father would provide the capital he needed to purchase inventory for the prospectors. He'd already placed his first order of pans, picks, shovels and axes. They were due to arrive by cargo ship within the month. If all went well, his shop would be ready within a few weeks of arriving in town.

Goldie and Lola glanced at one another with interest as he detailed his strategy.

"We'd love to visit your shop once you're all set up. Our business plans are in the making, and we'll be needing supplies." Goldie said, flashing her bright smile.

"You just let me know what you need, ma'am. I'll make sure to get you your merchandise at a fair price."

"Splendid."

The friends chattered with the newcomer while Donnie sat back and grinned, relieved they enjoyed his friend's company as much as he did. Jeremiah would glance up every so often, holding his best friend's gaze, along with a soft smile.

❦

MR. SMITH WAS A MAN OF MANY TALENTS. AS WELL AS AN ASTUTE BUSINESS sense, he possessed a broad understanding of the arts. When time permitted, he'd join Donnie by the water's edge, bringing along his canvas and sketchbooks.

They'd sit by the quiet currents, taking in the light as they captured the fleeting moment with paintbrush and pencil. Their friendship grew over time, lending itself to mutual attraction which blossomed one evening under a moonlit sky. Once they'd shared their first kiss, the young lovers realized they were destined to spend their lives together.

So, after much discussion and planning, they decided to move together to San Francisco and open the mercantile store. Three days passed before the couple summoned up the courage to share their plans with Donnie's parents. The Beckers listened, and when they'd finished, they sat a moment in contemplation. The father stood up from his chair, eyes locked on Jeremiah. He walked over and shook his hand, welcoming him to the family.

❦

SO, IT WAS BITTERSWEET WHEN THE FRIENDS TRAVELED THROUGH IDAHO, several hundred miles away from their final destinations. They tried to prepare for their farewell by spending as much time as they could together. A lush landscape awaited as they traveled up the Bear Lake Valley from Clover

Creek, intersecting with Soda Springs, a natural wonder which offered relief to the exhausted travelers.

Breathing in the odor of sulfa, the travelers gazed in wonderment at the foaming waters rising from the therapeutic pools.

Lola's girls were the first ones to try them out, splashing and giggling in the bubbling springs. Their enthusiasm was contagious, and they soon found themselves surrounded by their friends. Cathy helped Shane into the warm currents, sighing in relief. They tried not to think of their future goodbyes.

Following a two-day break, the caravan left the tranquil valley, much to the reluctance of the group, and headed to Fort Hall to load up on supplies for the California Trail. Shortly after leaving the outpost, the Oregon and California trails connected and then separated into northwesterly and southwesterly directions. For those parting, tears were shed, and travelers embraced, saying their final goodbyes. Once the Oregon-bound passengers moved on, the remaining group realized they'd probably never see their friends again. They were subdued for the next few days, trying to adjust to the new changes. Sadly, there wouldn't be time to mourn their losses. Unbeknownst to them, the time had come to *see the elephant.*

Chapter Twenty-Seven

Years later, when Cathy was older and wiser, she'd think back on the last few weeks of travel along the California Trail and shudder. For her, this was an incredibly difficult part of the journey. The merciless heat of the Sierra Nevada Desert and the numerous river crossings taxed her very soul. She would have nightmares about the experience for the remainder of her life, often waking up covered in sweat while her husband comforted her from the night terrors.

Travelers often referred to the experience as *seeing the elephant*. The colorful metaphor signified the pioneers' excitement in heading west, but also meant the ordeal was tainted by hardship and disappointment. Few people could boast they'd "seen the elephant," but for those who did, the experience wasn't something they'd want to face again.

The trail was overwhelming, but they'd overcome the challenge. As terrible as the desert was, they made it to the San Francisco Bay one foggy afternoon. The cool ocean air was invigorating, a welcome relief since covering miles of dry wastelands.

The friends shed many tears that day as they said their final farewells. Before they parted, Darla took Cathy aside privately.

"I want to thank you for your kindness on the trail. You gave me hope I might have a chance at a happy life. My darling popped the question last night." She flashed her sparkling engagement ring. "Bought this for me at Fort Hall...isn't it a beauty!"

"Oh, simply gorgeous. I'm so happy for you both."

Goldie and Lola put their arms around Cathy, Rachel and Simone. They huddled within the circle, reluctant to part ways.

"Girls, let's make a promise we'll always stay in touch," Cathy said. Her body trembled as they tried to say goodbye. Lola and Goldie fought back tears as they regarded their friend. Rachel smiled down at the cooing baby in her arms. "You always have a place in my heart. I'm grateful for your help bringing my little Isaac into the world."

Cat caressed the child's mop of curly blond hair, blinking away tears. When they'd said their final farewells, she handed out slips of paper with her new address. Lola took hers and immediately pushed it down her brassiere.

Donnie and Jeremiah took Cathy aside privately to say their goodbyes.

"I'd love for you to visit us sometime. We plan to open our new store, *Becker and Smith Mercantile*, within the next few weeks. There's going to be a little boutique in the back...so if yah ever want to bring your dresses for sale, we'd be more than happy to put them up for commission."

Cathy took her friend's hands, looking deep into his eyes. "I'm so proud of you, Donnie. I know you will be a success in whatever business you choose. We're so grateful for all the hard work driving the wagon and helping out at the cooking fire."

"We want to give you something for your time," Shane said. He handed the boy an envelope full of cash.

Donnie blushed as he took the money.

"Thank you. My pleasure."

Jeremiah offered a smile, his eyes full of love. Cathy realized their relationship was quite serious. She was thrilled they'd found happiness together with the support of their family.

Donnie's parents openly wept as they said goodbye to their son, embracing him tightly before leaving, promising to visit their shop before the year's end.

So, despite the hardships along the trail, Cathy and her friends persevered and were able to focus on the final moments of travel with optimism. They clung to their dreams as they crossed the last miles of their journey, knowing they'd *seen the elephant* and lived to tell about it.

Chapter Twenty-Eight

AFTER CROSSING THE NEVADA DESERT, THE COOL OCEAN AIR OF THE Central Valley was a welcome relief. The sea stretched endlessly before them like a breathtaking mirage. Paradise was close, even if they couldn't quite grasp the reality of it.

The newlyweds drove separate wagons since parting with their friends heading to San Francisco. They followed the directions from their letter, traveling over the sandy shores of Monterey with its lush hills carpeted in striking ice plants and swirling sand dunes.

The Pacific Ocean was magnificent, waves pummeling together under the setting sun. They drove down to the cliffside overlooking the tides, parking their wagons by a weather-worn barn. By this time, Shane was able to maneuver his crutches quite easily and went to work untethering the teams. There was plenty of room for both the mules and horses inside the spacious stalls, knee-deep with fresh straw. Midnight, the raven, followed them inside, landing on a crossbeam over the manger. He ruffled his feathers and began preening in the fading light.

"Looks like he's making himself at home."

"I think he's going to like it here. Noticed quite a few ravens flying around near the beach when we drove up. Perhaps he'll find a lady friend."

"I wouldn't be surprised."

The couple finished putting out hay and grain for the animals as they neighed and hawed in anticipation. Once they were set up, the couple strolled down a foot-worn path.

They stopped for a moment, studying their new home. The cottage was a cozy whitewashed structure with a weathered tin roof framed by flower boxes hanging beneath lace-curtained windows. Colorful pansies filled the rustic planters, while a matching picket fence surrounded the modest yard.

"The house is so beautiful." Her husband nodded in agreement while opening the front gate, dropping his crutches in the process.

"Oh, be careful, you'll hurt yourself!"

Shane chuckled with a glimmer in his eyes, then to Cathy's amazement, gathered her up in his powerful arms, carrying her to the front door and over the threshold.

She stared in disbelief. "How on earth?"

'My leg's been better the last couple of weeks."

He gave her a kiss before placing her onto the hardwood floor.

"This is so lovely. I can't believe we're home."

She looked about the room in astonishment. Her hand grazed over the dining room table, admiring the green and white checkered tablecloth. A crystal vase rested on top, filled with bright pink roses. Shane reached for a note folded next to the flowers and read the words aloud.

Dear Shane and Cathy,

Please make yourself comfortable. There's wood in the fireplace and some bread, cheese and wine in the kitchen. We'd love to have you over for supper once you're settled in. My husband and I look forward to meeting you both. I will never be able to thank you enough for taking such good care of my parents. You'll always be part of our family.

With Love,

Mable

The newlyweds smiled after reading the letter, looking about their new house in wonder. The cottage was everything they could hope for following their long trek. Shane walked to the tiny kitchen against the back wall, opening a cupboard next to the sink which groaned loudly on its hinges. Reaching inside, he retrieved two glasses, then uncorked a bottle of red wine on the counter. He poured them each a drink, raising his glass for a toast.

"To my beautiful wife, I'm ready to share a life full of love and adventure with you. Well…love's more than enough…come to think of it. We've experienced a world of adventure already."

"Agreed."

Cat giggled as she took a sip from her glass. The liquid warmed her from the inside, and she sighed contently, considering his handsome face.

Shane reached for his wife's hand, kissing it softly, then turned toward the fireplace. She savored her wine while glancing over his chiseled form, amazed at how nicely he'd recovered over the last few weeks.

Outside the wind whipped against the sides of the cottage as the waves crashed along the shore. A harvest moon sent soft beams of light dancing through the open windows. Once the fire was glowing in the hearth, he stepped closer, taking her small hands in his.

"I love you, Mrs. Mackenzie."

"I love you, too, Mr. Mackenzie." She let out a sigh as she gazed into his cool grey eyes.

"There's a little secret I've been keeping from you."

"Oh?"

Dimples formed in the corners of his mouth as he offered a lopsided grin.

"I've been able to walk without crutches for over a week now." His eyes twinkled in the firelight.

Cathy's mouth fell open in astonishment.

"Why didn't you tell me?"

He bit down on the corner of his lip before answering. "Well, I figured we were so close to home and…I wanted our first time to be special. Thought you might like a roof over your head."

The corners of her mouth rose, as her eyes filled with tears.

"You're the sweetest man, Mr. Mackenzie."

He chuckled, gathering her up in his arms as if she weighed nothing.

"Well, it hasn't been easy, my love. I've been waiting a very long time."

"Me, too."

His mouth rose in the corners, eyes glistening as he lowered her down across the four-poster bed.

She sighed, stretching across the soft mattress, a luxury after sleeping for months inside the wagon. Logs crackled in the cheery hearth as thunder boomed overhead, shaking the beams of the cottage to its foundation. Rain pelted the windows while a fierce wind shook the paned glass. As she gazed into his loving eyes, she realized she was finally home.

Lightning flashed outside, filling the cottage with a brilliant glow, causing Cathy to jump

in surprise. Shane pulled her close, kissing her warm lips.

"I'll always keep you safe, darlin'."

"I know, love. You always have."

His eyes shone with passion as he considered her trembling body, his hands caressing over shapely curves.

"Are you sure, Shane?" Your ribs…"

He gazed into her wide eyes.

"My ribs will be fine."

He waited in anticipation, white teeth flashing in the soft light. She removed his shirt, and soon the rest of his clothes were tumbling to the floor.

The corners of his mouth pulled up as he moved her body closer, steel-gray eyes glimmering in the darkness. Passionate kisses became more urgent as his fingers caressed the hollow of her neck, moving toward the buttons of her dress. Taking his time, he released each one, exposing delicate flesh. His lips grazed over her breasts as she shivered in the shadows. Outside, a bolt of lightning dashed across the starless sky, followed by a roll of thunder in the distance. Waves pummeled together like battling titans. The wind moaned and shook the cabin's beams in fierce gusts.

Cathy barely noticed the raging storm outside the cabin's walls. She was enraptured by Shane's touch and time stood still. The firelight flickered, casting soft beams across their faces, eyes burning with passion like fire behind glass. She felt his hands undressing her, fingers grazing over the contours of her silky skin. A scattering of goosebumps surfaced as the cold wind made its way into the open spaces of their cottage. He kissed the bumps ever so softly, lips warming the delicate mounds of her breasts, tongue flicking over nipples hardening to his touch. She let out a soft moan, running her fingers through his wavy hair.

He smiled at her eagerness and placed his hand under the small of her back, moving closer. Cat's body was now throbbing for him with an urgent need, never yearning for anything as she did in this moment and was quite ready to be indulged. Shane intended to satisfy her every fantasy and looked forward to taking his time doing so. His hand reached down, caressing her inner thigh, inches from her aching desire. He hesitated, gazing longingly into her emerald eyes.

Yes, my love.

His eyes glistened as the corners of his mouth rose. He reached down, grazing over her delicate skin, then with a bit more pressure until she moaned in ecstasy, begging for more. He smiled down, eyes burning with desire. As she quivered in anticipation, he caressed her hips, flickering his tongue inside her eager mouth, teasing her as his lips traveled over her neck, breasts and belly, warming her every curve. She raked her fingers through his wavy locks, sighing with pleasure, pulling him closer as her legs trembled uncontrollably. He gazed in wonder; eyes filled with longing. There were no interruptions as the newlyweds discovered one another. Shane took his time, satisfying Cathy's every desire until she couldn't take it anymore. She cried out his name, ready for the secret to be revealed. As he entered tenderly, their bodies became one by the glow of the firelight. The storm raged on as the young lovers moved through space and time, their passion igniting as the waves hit the shore.

WHEN THEY'D EXHAUSTED THEMSELVES IN PEACEFUL SURRENDER, CATHY snuggled against her husband as he gazed down with a soft smile.

"I love you, little Cat. God, you're the most beautiful woman I've ever laid eyes on. You truly are my heart and soul." He kissed her full lips, holding her close in his arms as the rain pelted down over the tin-covered roof. His fingers brushed back the ebony locks from her damp forehead. She gazed up into loving eyes, snuggling close against his chest. "Shane, I'll love you forever. You're my everything."

They laid together in the firelight, caressing one another as the storm raged on, an undeniable love which would last the test of time.

The Legacy

THE MACKENZIE'S WOULD SPEND THE REST OF THEIR LIVES TOGETHER IN THE cabin by the sea. Shane worked his way up in the Becker's rancho and was able to provide quite nicely for his family. Cathy opened a shop downtown, and her dress boutique was soon the talk of the town. They saved their money, and over time, they were able to join their friends for occasional visits to San Francisco. The ladies were thrilled to show them their city and all the exciting wonders of the Barbary Coast.

The women kept to their promise, writing letters to each other for the rest of their lives. Each new correspondence told a story rich with adventure, romance and sometimes tragedy. Lola and Goldie both suffered losses from fires, natural disasters and man-made dangers during the wild days of the *Barbary Coast*. Yet, they always found the strength to rebuild, becoming successful businesswomen despite their struggles.

She was happy to hear how Donnie and Jeremiah made quite the life together, opening a successful mercantile store on O'Farrell Street in the heart of the financial district. Donnie also became a well-known dress designer. His seamstress work was sought after from the elite ladies in town, as well as his artworks, showing paintings at a popular San Francisco gallery called *The Muse*.

The strong-willed Madame opened a well-known cathouse—a famous pink-painted building named *Lola's Ladies*. Her girls wore their new gowns in the grand opening, much to the delight of their wealthy clientele. Over time, the business became the most popular brothel in San Francisco, earning the attentions of both businessman and politician alike.

Fiery red-headed Dottie left *Lola's Ladies* to start her own dynasty catering to a less affluent crowd. Becoming a success in her own right, her establishment grew over time, earning her both independence and financial freedom.

Goldie's empire began with a simple canvas tent filled with makeshift tables, chairs and sawhorses. Men would line up for hours outside, waiting for their chance to glimpse the most beautiful card dealer in San Francisco. Over time, the modest business grew into a finely built two-story gambling hall named *The Golden Queen*. The golden-haired beauty never married or raised a family, investing all her time and soul within her profitable business. She took the occasional lover, but never fully committed, much to the disappointment of her many admirers.

Darla embraced a quieter life, settling down with her new husband Isaac Collins and their three children. His carpentry business was quite profitable, so they branched out with their new business partner Mr. Jacob Levy. The company turned a nice profit, earning them a place within the high society crowd of San Francisco. Darla was well-liked in her community, hosting popular quilting bees and elaborate parties, becoming involved in the Suffrage movement later in life. The family moved into an elegant *Painted Lady* a popular Victorian architecture style known as the *Queen Anne*. Her fairytale-looking home was painted canary yellow, bubblegum pink and soft lilac, making it stand out from her neighbors' like an enormous Easter egg.

Rachel Cohen purchased a more subdued Victorian a few houses down with her husband and grown children. Mr. Cohen became a successful banker, passing down the business to his three sons. The families were overjoyed to be neighbors once again, embracing their twilight years in comfort and leisure, often reminiscing about the *good old days* along the trail.

Over the years, Shane and Cathy were blessed with two beautiful children. The lovers grew old together, living to see their grandchildren and great-grandchildren playing along the white beaches of Monterey.

When Cathy was in her seventies, she decided to write down her trail experiences within the pages of a gold-bound diary. Her beloved children cherished the book as their most treasured heirloom. Along with the story, the cabin remained in the family over the decades, passed along to each new generation. Their love would never be forgotten, embraced forever in the hearts and minds of the Mackenzie clan.

Epilogue

JADE MACKENZIE WHISPERED A PRAYER FOR HER MOTHER.

The cool ocean breeze blew sandy blond locks around a heart-shaped face, while tears fell from steel-grey eyes. She walked along the mossy trail, glancing over the grounds of the *Queen of Heaven Cemetery*. The girl watched as a seagull landed atop a marble statue of the Virgin Mary, squabbling up at the darkening sky. Turning her back, she hurried across the manicured lawn toward her vehicle, pressing the key fob. The door clicked open with a sharp beep, and she climbed inside the chilly Ford pickup.

With her wipers on high, she drove down highway 101 heading to Monterey. An icy wind sent goosebumps over her body, so she flipped on the heat. She passed miles of sand dunes and colorful ice plants, the waves crashing together along the beach, foamy peaks rising from the glassy currents. Sea lions stretched lazily along granite boulders, basking in the fleeting rays of the setting sun. Thunder boomed overhead, the afternoon sky darkening eerily over the valley.

Her mind drifted as she drove, glancing toward the glovebox, considering the new deed. She parked her truck behind the cottage, grabbed her purse, diary and bag of groceries, then slipped down onto the sandy beach. Seagulls cried, diving toward the raging waters. Jade stopped a moment, gazing at the shoreline, watching the garnet rays fading toward the horizon. She walked up the cobblestone path to the front of the modest cottage, briefly noticing the weather-worn exterior. She ran her finger over the course boards peeling off a few flakes of paint in the process. There was quite a lot of work to do fixing up the old place, along with opening her antique shop in Pacific Grove. Juggling both projects at once seemed like a daunting task. Taking a deep breath, her hand reached toward the copper knob; then her key clicked into place. She pushed the door open with a groan to its hinges. At the same moment, streaks of lightning flashed above as a white missile shot past her right side, landing by her feet in a blur of snowy feathers.

She gasped, reaching her hand toward the injured bird fluttering on its side. The creature thrashed the ground, trying in vain to fly, the right wing bent at a startling angle. His pale eyes caught her gaze, and she knew in an instant what she must do. Cradling him close, she scooped him up, making her way inside the darkness.

The cottage was musty and in need of a good cleaning. Old books and vintage collectibles layered in thick dust cluttered about the room. A wire basket sat in the corner by the hearth, so she placed it on the bed, then pulled her scarf from her neck and lined the bottom. After examining the injury, she wrapped the wing in place with a piece of linen from the sewing box. Satisfied with her doctoring, she placed the baby raven inside the basket. She studied the bird in astonishment, not quite sure what to make of him. He appeared healthy, other than his injured wing, but his feathers, which should have been ebony in color, were shockingly white. The fledgling nibbled the soft material, then fluffed his feathers and began to preen, eyes fixed on his new mother. Within a few minutes, he surrendered to sleep inside the makeshift nest. She looked at her charge with a soft smile, then moved toward the fireplace starting the logs with a lighter and bit of old newspaper. She sighed as the room warmed and shadows receded to the far corners of the room.

Rain pounded the tin roof, as the wind rattled the windows in their vintage frames. She looked around, listening to the fire crackling in the hearth; *everything was old, yet so familiar.*

Once she'd kicked off her shoes and put away the groceries, she opened a bottle of local Chardonnay and poured herself a generous glass. Outside, the storm raged, shaking the cottage to its foundations. Thunder boomed, a lightning flashed behind lace curtains. Taking a seat at the edge of the bed she reached for the gold-leaf diary. For the next several hours, she traveled back in time, enraptured by her ancestor's journey. Turning the final page released a pearly white feather which slipped from the binding. Jade held it up to the firelight in wonder, tears blurring her vision. As she considered the snowy quill, she realized her story was only beginning.

THE END

Don't miss out on your next favorite book!

Join the Satin Romance mailing list
www.satinromance.com/mail.html

About the Author

AnneMarie Dapp is a graduate of San Francisco State University, where she studied Studio Arts and Art History. She lives and writes on Sock Monkey Ranch, her and her husband Dale's vegan farm in Prunedale, California.

https://sockmonkey.live

facebook.com/AnneMarieDapp68

twitter.com/AnneMarieDapp

instagram.com/annemariedapp

pinterest.com/duckmomma1

CPSIA information can be obtained
at www.ICGtesting.com
Printed in the USA
LVHW041506040520
654951LV00004B/1043

9 781680 468724